VETERAN

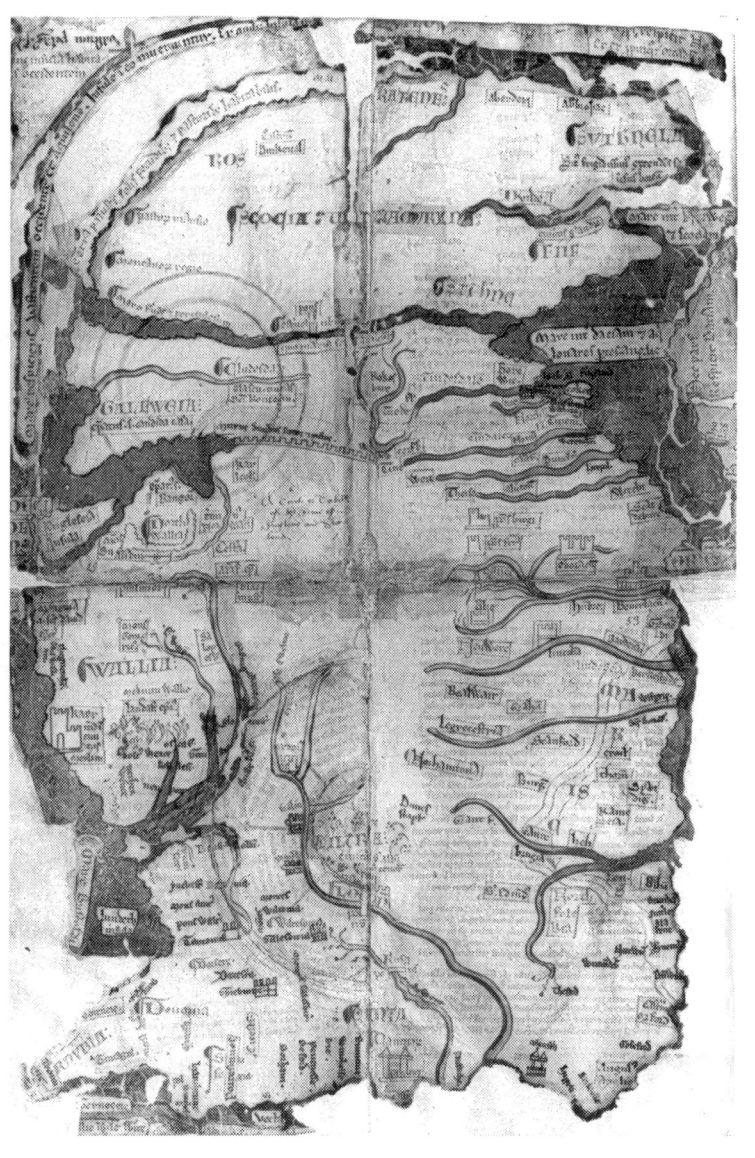

Map of England by Matthew Paris, thirteenth century

'If everything on earth were rational, nothing would happen.'

Dostoyevsky, *The Brothers Karamazov*, translated David Magarshak, Penguin 1957, quoted in *The Real Meaning of Money* by Dorothy Rowe

Veteran

E W S Ashton

OSWESTRY LONGDEN

Copyright © E W S Ashton 2000
First published in 2000 by Oswestry Longden
Longden
22 Morda Close
Oswestry, Shropshire SY11 2BA

Distributed by Gazelle Book Services Limited,
Falcon House, Queen Square,
Lancaster, England LA1 1RN

British Library Cataloguing in Publication Data
A catalogue record for this book is available from the British Library

ISBN 0-9538005-0-4

Typeset by Amolibros, Watchet, Somerset
This book production has been managed by Amolibros
Printed and bound by T J International Ltd, Padstow, Cornwall,
England

Acknowledgements

Who's Who in Early Medieval England by Christopher Tyerman, Shepheard-Walwyn, London.

Line drawings in the book supplied by Gordon Redrup.

Medieval map on pages 98-99 drawn by the author.

Pilgrims' Map, London to Dover, page 7, supplied courtesy of the British Library.

Jacket illustration, repeated on page iii, supplied courtesy of the British Library, MS COTTON JUL D.VII. FOLS 50-53.

Contents

Preface

Two subjects interested me most when I decided to start this book.

The first was concerned with the problem of finding your way around in the twelfth century when there were no road maps, few could read and there were no signposts.

And the second, with regard to the events of that time, were the questions which had cropped up frequently during my career as an industrialist and development engineer, "What really happened?" and "Can a cause be identified?"

The matter of finding your way around without being able to read was once brought to my attention when an elderly driver who could neither read nor write was sent from my factory in the north of England with a load of machinery for my French factory. We had a new transport manager and he was not familiar with the drivers, so David was given the job and being the man he was he just accepted it and set off.

The only incident in what must have been an interesting journey that I heard about was that David went the wrong way round the only roundabout in Northern France. Otherwise there was nothing to report.

But as most journeys in the twelfth century were on foot, or sometimes on horseback, the traveller had far better contact with his world than does the modern car driver. Some idea of his orientation would be always with him and there were passers-by to ask. I once had a job thrust upon me, of visiting fifty depots scattered throughout the British Isles and the best way I found of not getting regularly lost (say in south London, or mid-Birmingham or central Glasgow) was to install a little compass in my car.

I give here two maps, kindly indicated to me by Brian Hopper of the Royal Commission on the Historical Monuments of England, that show the state of map-making in the early Middle Ages.

The first is Matthew Paris's map drawn in the scriptorium of St Albans Abbey in the thirteenth century showing the whole of Britain, and the second shows pilgrims' maps of the London to Dover road.

It is still not easy to work out how anyone could set off with confidence from Southampton with the idea of getting to York!

Turning now to "What really happened?" a surprising number of professional people spend their time trying to solve this problem, barristers and coroners being two examples.

For me as an industrialist and engineer, post-mortems were a regular thing: sometimes trying to find out why a few thousand items had all been sold with one important dimension wrong; or why a certain product had failed when a customer insisted that the way he used it had been perfectly normal; or again what had actually gone on between a salesman and a customer who we had lost.

And as a research hydrodynamicist in my early days, when repeating a classical piece of experimentation, I found that the standard paper on the subject had left out certain important aberrations to make the result tidier (the aberrations being of considerable importance later). I realised that even with a relatively simple situation, with few variables, the utmost care is required if important matters are not to be left out.

My book is about the time of King Stephen about whom Christopher Tyerman in his book, *Who's Who in Early Medieval England,* wrote:

'Stephen of Blois (c1096-1154; King of England 1135-1154) is chiefly remembered as an unsuccessful king, whose reign formed a chaotic interlude between the masterful rule of Henry I and Henry II. The damning verdict of the Peterborough version of the Anglo-Saxon Chronicle has stuck; "People said openly that Christ and his saints slept." English historians and their audience prefer strong kings, whatever their cost in terms of misery. For eight and a half centuries Stephen, who eminently failed to control events, has received short shrift. Yet it is not entirely obvious that conditions in England, when viewed from a perspective other than that of royal government or hostile and judgmental monastic chroniclers, were markedly worse than under more effective monarchs. Devastation was local, confined to areas most affected by civil war..."

And later in the same piece;

'...in the twelfth century, as in other centuries, nice people rarely make effective rulers".

There must be a distinct possibility that Stephen's forbearance and skilful manoeuvring prevented a countrywide bloodbath such as we have recently seen in Kosova, where "strong men" demonstrated their power by destroying most of the country.

During Stephen's nineteen years' reign, life carried on as normal in Britain. Cathedrals continued to be built, packhorse trains operated and windmills were introduced.

Full-scale war, for which the ingredients were certainly present and which might have set the country back fifty years, was avoided.

Perhaps if our forebears had had more facts about his reign, other than from highly biased churchmen with their personal and well staffed scriptoria, we ourselves would have been taught that Stephen was one of the greater kings in English history, one who kept the country going forward at a time when one with his background and training could have made a great name for himself on the battlefield.

INTRODUCTION

How the Ancient Document was Discovered

Haymaking time had come again but with the difference, which we found it hard to accept, that it would be our last. My brother and I had grown up on the hill farm and knew every ditch and tree. We had worked through bitter, wet days in winter to rebuild its stone walls and had tended sheep in every one of its corners and sheltered hollows. We had dug into wind-hardened snowdrifts with frozen hands for sheep trapped in February blizzards and stayed with them through pitch-black rainy nights at lambing time. While there was always something urgent and interesting, a life in itself very fitting for two strong healthy boys, our father had other ideas and insisted on school and homework, and the perusal of syllabuses and college courses, so that at seventeen (my brother at eighteen) I left home to study, in large cities.

We were bright, and did well and roamed far, but each year, from whenever we were, we returned to our old home for 'haytime'. With better machines as the years rolled on, there was less need, but it was a custom to be treasured, one we had no wish to break. Now our father was dead, two years before, and our mother was to move to a small house in the village. The farm dead stock had been sold and a price for the flock agreed with the incoming tenant.

1

Our hay-time visit had not been easy to keep for the last few years for either of us. My brother now lived in California and worked at the university there in the library of ancient manuscripts as head of the materials laboratory, and for a number of years I had been lecturer in Anglo-Saxon at the University of Toronto. We had both taken the hay-time commitment seriously, however, and each had a flexible holiday arrangement written into his contract. The Dean of my Faculty had pointed out that the drafting of the clause in my contract had cost the university 5000 Canadaian dollars in lawyers' fees.

On this, our last visit, there had been a run of those magic summer days, warm, sunny and with a gentle breeze, which occasionally surprise the farmers in the higher Pennines, and at mid-afternoon, on a day in mid-July, we found ourselves 'worked-up' – and near the 'New Barn'.

This ancient stone building, called 'new' perhaps in the same way that the English will often refer to a tall man as 'Tiny', or a miserable man as 'Happy', is about half a mile from the farmhouse, on the last pasture before the moor proper. Once, when a boy, climbing high up in the roof timbers to look at a kestrel's nest, I saw, cut in the beam, the letters 'HCB', followed by the date '1553', perhaps some evidence of the great age of the building.

My brother and I had known for many years – perhaps since we first helped with the hay and jumped on the stack as it grew high within the barn – that where the flagged roof joined the thick rubble end walls, near the peak, there was an upright flagstone set into the wall in a curious way. It had once been plastered, perhaps to hide it, but the plaster had mostly dropped off over the years. It seemed to be immovable but had so much the appearance of a cupboard door that my brother and I had often prodded it, when the stack had reached its top level and we were able once again to look at it, without making any impression. It remained 'on the agenda', as we would say in later life, but we always intended to have a good look at it 'one day'. We called it in our chatter 'the cupboard in the old barn'.

On this sunny July afternoon, a little sleepy and tired after ten days' haymaking, it struck us both at the same time that this would be the last chance to explore 'the cupboard'. A ladder had been left after mending a flag on the roof of the barn and we had a crowbar in the tractor. 'Come on, let's have a last look,' said my brother.

We had stacked the hay, in rectangular bales, away from the barn wall this year, and we could lean a ladder against the wall with its end almost against the cupboard.

Dan climbed up and I was close behind, carrying the crowbar. He tried to move the slab with his hands, as we had tried many times before but nothing moved and I passed him the crowbar. He first inserted the sharp heel in a crack on the left side and levered, at first gently, and then as hard as his rocky perch on the ladder would allow. Nothing moved. Then he changed the bar to the right-hand side of the slab and again levered gently. Without difficulty the slab moved a little to the left and left a small opening. At that moment our torch failed and we got down and went home, having seen nothing to make us excited.

Our curiosity had been rekindled, however, so that two days later we returned with a freshly charged torch. Further efforts at the top of the shaky ladder opened the door about three inches and although it then stuck firm we were able to shine the torch inside and see that it was indeed a shallow cupboard, with a pile of dust and rubble lying on its floor. It was a natural thing for me to do (I was at the top of the ladder at that time, Dan had had to go down with a coughing attack from the dust) – to stretch in and finger the rubble. I felt a bundle of a different texture to the stones and rubble, pulled it out, slipped it into my pocket and climbed down.

I walked into the sunshine, where Dan was recovering, and we looked at my find. When the dust had been shaken off, we saw it to be a parcel, nine inches long by three inches square, wrapped in a kind of skin. 'Vellum,' said my brother (he handled such stuff daily, in his work). 'Made from local sheepskin. We will have to be very careful with it. Is there anything else?'

I climbed the ladder again and reached into the recess and felt a smooth, hard object among the small stones and plaster debris. I climbed down with it.

Just as we walked out through the barn door to look at this other object, our neighbour rode up on his Suzuki and as he

4

drew near we could see that something was wrong. Calling at the farmhouse, he had met Dr Jinnen coming out through the door who told him that when he had entered, this being one of his regular visits, he had found our mother dead in her chair.

There followed a sad and confusing time for both of us. We had to return to our jobs in another continent in a few days and yet had to clear up the affairs of three generations in the old farmhouse. The finds from the 'cupboard' were pushed into out respective suitcases, Dan taking the 'vellum', I the hard metal object, and we struggled hard with the local auctioneer and our mother's lawyer to tidy up her estate.

To move to the final destination of our two finds, the metal object turned out to be a small crucifix, made by the twelfth century York lost-wax process, with a border of most delicately arranged rubies. It now lies in its own case, beautifully illuminated, in the British Museum.

The vellum is also carefully preserved in York Museum, not displayed, so as to avoid light damage, but with a facsimile available for scholars. I have my own copy, made by my brother, using one of his own processes which avoided any damage to the original, and it is this copy I have used to transcribe the writings of a long-dead priest to form this book. The writings on the vellum were as follows.

The first sheet was written out in full, in a form of Latin that I could understand although there were many difficult abbreviations and corruptions. It went as follows.

'An account of a journey through England, during the uprisings and disruptions in the reign of King Stephen, undertaken by Edwin, an old soldier returning from France to his birthplace in Northern Yorkshire. Written by Father Riveaux in the year of our Lord 1170. The special form of this account is for the following reasons.

Over a number of years I had grown to know Edwin well and had become aware of his skill in describing situations in which he had found himself during a very active life. I had also become aware that the terrible problems and uprisings that occurred during Stephen's reign were beginning to be forgotten, as our Noble and Mighty King Henry the Second succeeds in raising the spirits of his nation to new heights. I therefore had a deep wish to set down Edwin's experiences, but vellum was scarce and expensive and I was a poor parish priest.

Then I thought of a way, having managed to obtain a pile of vellum trimmings from the vellum-maker in York. I would set down a condensed version of the story in a short form of writing, which had been suggested long ago by Anselm, which takes up not a twentieth of the space of normal script. (Anselm said it was the form used by Julius Caesar.) Moreover, this 'picture writing' is independent of language so that a Latin scholar might transcribe it in Latin, or one more used to the vernacular could write it out in that language. I have included a list of some five score signs, with their equivalents in Latin to make translation easier. I ask whosoever attempts to transcribe these notes to forgive the unscholarly paths along which I have been forced, for the sake of brevity, in attempting this exercise.

When I came to transcribe the notes it was particularly inconvenient that the writer had either forgotten to enclose the 'five score signs and their Latin equivalents', or that they had been mislaid. Because of this there are many more of my own imaginative guesses than the original writer, obviously a man of some exactness, would have wished. However I found so many interesting points concerning the history of those far-away times that I do not hesitate to offer this transcription, full of approximations as it is, to the general reader. Scholars of the period will no doubt wish to form their own judgements about the meaning of some of the 'pictures' after examining the original document.

How the document and the crucifix came to be hidden in the cupboard is impossible to tell, but several times in our long history church treasures have had to be concealed if they

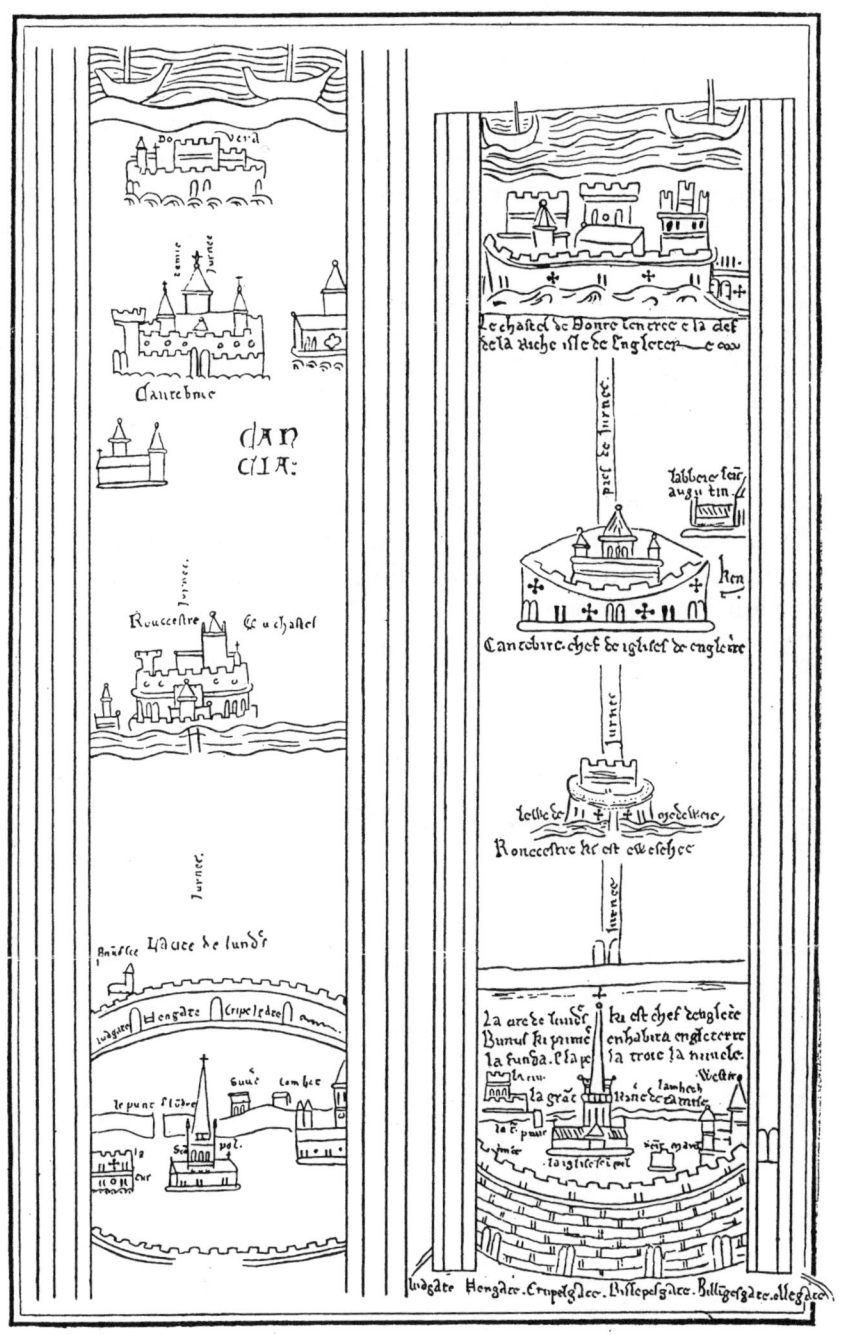

Section of Pilgrim's Map, London to Dover

7

were to survive. Some piles of stones on a hillside across from our farm, the remains of an ancient building, have long been called 'The Old Nunnery', and it is easy to imagine the mother superior, under threat of sacking by Henry the Eighth's soldiers, creeping up to the barn at night and placing her two most precious possessions in the cupboard. But what was the cupboard made for in the first place? And why was the bundle of vellum trimmings regarded as precious?

I had been working on the notes of the old priest for two years before I finally abandoned any idea of attempting a precise translation. The historian in me preached the main danger of imprecision, that the gap between imprecision and falsity is very narrow, and I knew that I had an important document in my hands. Nevertheless I decided to set down what I thought the old priest was trying to say and in the end I found enough new material, albeit often vague and imprecise, to have made the work worthwhile and I trust the reader will be left with the same impression.

So we move to Edwin's tale, as set down by the priest.

CHAPTER ONE

About the Priest and Edwin

I was walking down the street after baptising Maud, our young blacksmith's second daughter, when he came round the bend from the road. We exchanged 'Good-days' and he asked me the way to the hovel of Dancer, who he said was his second cousin.

Today Maud would have been eleven if she had not died five days ago of a great pain in her belly, and as I went on with her funeral I remembered meeting Edwin, that first time, half way through Stephen's reign, a reign which we thought would never end.

Everybody now calls him 'Veteran' even though his given name is Edwin. In fact 'Halfa' was the first name he got, because our young men, asking how many men he had killed when a-soldiering, were told, 'Half a man'. Then he went on to tell them that, in the great fight at Tinchebraie (his first battle, he was only a boy), he and a mate speared one of Duke Robert's short-sword men and claimed 'half' each.

He is big-built and wide, below normal height. He stands very straight. He is direct in both his look and his speech as if thirty years in the military have trained him to face up to anything that life can throw at him. Although he is not one to push forward and not of our inner court, he is often asked for his ideas, particularly on matters of war and fighting, of which we saw something and heard a lot during the miserable and wasteful reign of King Stephen, now happily ended.

In the military he became a builder in big timbers and stone through working on defence posts and small castles, and his knowledge and experience of the machines of war is also great. A model mangonel, very carefully made, which could throw a small stone one hundred paces was his gift to our boy-squire two or three months after he arrived. Its twisted skein was made from a bundle of hairs from the tail of one of Banard's cows.

Because of his skills he has found plenty to occupy him in the manor, particularly when large buildings have had to be roofed, like the extension to our church two years ago.

I myself have been priest of this village of Tentwell for a long time, perhaps forty-five years, depending on the 'vacant period' when the Archbishop of York fought the Bishop of Durham over the rights to appoint clerics here. During those forty years I have not travelled further than York. That's very different, as I shall tell, from my experiences as a young man, and although I have been perfectly content with my lowly but demanding duties, I have never missed an opportunity to talk to travellers about their experiences in order to keep alive an interest in the wider world.

So after many talks with Edwin during his three years in Tentwell and finding him an alert watcher and an accurate raconteur I have had a scholarly urge to set down on vellum all that he saw in the course of the two years he wandered up the length of England during the reign of King Stephen. It was a troubled reign, sad and dangerous for all of us.

Even now I can never get him to talk about his military adventures in France and Spain. When I pressed him hard one evening he would only say that his military life had been generally peaceful with only a few short, frenzied and dangerous actions. While he has claimed only 'half a man' in the whole of his soldiering life (he finds this useful to turn the talk away from serious soldiering), he once told me that he had been very close to death on six occasions and that it was a mystery, over which he pondered sadly from time to time, how he himself managed to escape while his comrades died. In fact, his soldiering has left him puzzles that he has no way of solving.

It was mathematics which brought us close together, I a well-trained priest and he a long-serving soldier, with little else in common other than being both Yorkshire born. As I shall tell, the French University of Laon, where I was trained as a priest, had a tradition of mathematical training for all its students, so that I became proficient not only in arithmetic as used in accountancy but also in geometry as taught by the Arabs of the southern Mediterranean. Thus, many times have I been able to assist master builders in our locality with the geometry of their buildings. And Edwin himself had picked up considerable skill in practical arithmetic and geometry through his work in designing war machines and defence posts; it was his use of the word *parabola* when he was describing the use of the toy mangonel which drew me to him in the first place.

Even during our early talks I saw that the manner of his journey from Southampton to Yorkshire had given him time to look closely at many enterprises in England and that an account of his journey would be a significant historical record. Hence these writings.

This summer of 1155 has been warm and there has been much gossiping in the dusty street in the long evenings when light sometimes stays in our northern skies for the whole night. Now is a time when we all feel free to talk, with the second Henry on his way to restoring the 'King's Peace' of his grandfather.

In talking to Edwin on these fine evenings, he has agreed that I shall set down the story of his adventures in King Stephen's England, which I intend to do in spite of my eyesight being rather poor.

[Note in a spidery longhand along the edge of the vellum: On looking at the manuscript in the year of our Lord 1170 I cannot make out all that I wrote. News of Becket has just reached us. God preserve us from another civil war.]

Edwin's story starts after he had been landed at Southampton from a large French boat partly covered over with hurdles at the stern and very wet. His passage had been paid for by the Duke of Rouen in whose personal guard he had served for thirty years.

In a stupid mishap, involving fighting in a nunnery, he had lost his right hand – he who had come through at least five major battles and numberless skirmishes – as a heavy door was banged shut by the prioress. He had been in charge of the watch which surprised a party of drunken Flemish mercenaries as they pushed into the nunnery and he shoved out the last mercenary just as the prioress swung the heavy door shut, taking off the greater part of his right hand. The Duke's surgeon/ barber amputated the remainder and he was left with the stump of a forearm protected by a leather cup to which was riveted a metal hook.

Being now crippled as well as elderly, he was released from the Duke's army and his passage paid to England, with the right to keep his short sword and a present of ten marks from the Duke. He was not bitter about all this, his relief at being able to arrange his own life being compensation for his loss of security under the Duke and the loss of his hand.

I am starting to write this on the last day of October in the year 1170, the day in which Edwin was to join me in my cottage so that I could start recording his chronicles. A short time ago however his neighbour, Salter, a small farmer, called to say that Edwin's fever had come again and that he would not be able to come. This fever is what he calls his 'African fever', and it returns every few months for two or three days.

As he has not been able to come, and as I want to practise my writing in this new sign language, I will first set down my own story because no writer has ever set down another's tale without changing it to fit more nearly with his own experiences. Thus a man of simple habits and tastes, which I myself have been for many years now, my model being the good Archbishop Thurstan, will tend to shy away from complex experiences in his story, whereas a man of complex tastes will be inclined to complicate even the simplest of happenings. And I would have the reader know that I have long wrestled against the belief that all men's actions can be 'explained' in terms of primary tendencies, a thought which misses completely the fact that men frequently act without sense, against their own interests, in ways which can never be explained.

As well as mathematics, the unreasonable actions of Edwin during his journey were what brought us together in the telling of his tales. During one of our first talks, when he was describing his experiences in the Royal Forest in Hampshire, he said, in his forthright way, 'I really have no idea why I did that, at that time,' whereas many men would have brought in fate or the pagan gods (which still appeal to many), to add nothing, to an already empty explanation.

My own curiosity in the way that men will often behave without sense, against their better interest, has been with me for most of my life, starting with one mad act of my own, as a young man, which changed the course of my life and which I will shortly describe.

As I have grown to know Edwin it has became obvious that he excels as an observer, being always prepared to set his own opinions aside, at least in the first place. It has been very interesting for me to talk to someone prepared to give facts rather than opinions, but Edwin last week mentioned a most amazing thing, that he had actually attended lectures on Aristotle and his reasonings, given by the Duke's crippled brother to a class of 'Volunteers' from the castle guard at Rouen.

The act of stupidity which changed my own life took place when I was a student in the Monastery of Laon, at that time part of the University of Laon and the leading centre in all Christendom for training lay-orientated students. The *scholastici* of this school were very different from the *claustrali* of other monastic schools, most of the students being destined for governmental posts in the new-style courts of the French and English monarchies. I had been sent there for training by Archbishop Thomas of York, for whom my father had been able to do a small favour during the drafting of Domesday, and so rapid was my progress that I was working directly for the Abbot himself at the time of my downfall. Not only was I able to write French and Latin (and converse in each of them readily) as well as the dialect of this region, which I shall call English, but under the tutelage of the Abbott I had become an experienced enquirer into legal disputes and a trained reporter of such investigations. It was the Abbot who insisted that my reports to him should be free from opinions – a difficult requirement for an ambitious young man, because without the judgements which are claimed by a young man's conceits, his reports will seem to him empty indeed.

An understanding of mathematics, particularly that branch which dealt with the handling of money, was obligatory in the Abbey for all clerics, because the Abbot, who at all times laid emphasis on the need for precision, often preached numeracy as the path to the truth in human affairs.

Thus if we were reporting on the date of birth of a bastard son who might inherit a vast estate, we were taught to give only the known facts and not be tempted, say by the gossip of courtiers, to guess at an answer. I remember one such case, where the bastard was nearly sixty years old and all we could establish was that he had been born between the King's visit to Nancy in 1132 and his journey to the Holy Land, which started in January 1135. No witnesses could be found to say that they saw the baby before the first date, yet there were plenty who saw him after the second one. My report on that case was sent to His Holiness the Pope for his ruling.

The teaching of the Abbot built in many ways on the teachings of my own father about whom I must say a few things in explaining my own philosophies at that time in my life, and indeed later.

My father was the squire of a small manor in northern Yorkshire who led a relaxed but full life on his 400 acres. Much of the land was let off to four tenants in return for work on the estate and this gave him the time to pursue his two main hobbies of bow-making and the philosophical study of estate management. He was one of the few men in England who could make a long bow such as were used in southern Wales, and the vast superiority of the long bow over the usual short bow was one of his favourite topics. He found many connections between his bow developments and estate management and was fond of using the various aspects of the art of bow-making to illustrate how the management of an estate should be arranged.

For instance he was fond of saying, 'Don't waste time on poor wood,' which he sometimes expanded to explain that it was worth taking great care at the start of any enterprise so that future efforts would have a good foundation. With his bows, he would spend much time selecting the best pieces of wood (ash or willow) to be stored and dried. He was particularly careful with the seasoning of the wood (under cover but with good ventilation), so that in three or four years the hard work of shaping would be worthwhile. And he would use this simple advice to those who proposed to plant seed in poor ground or breed off an unsuitable animal. We were a male-household and I was much with my father. My mother had died at my birth and I was little in touch with women, nor have I been during my whole life.

From the Abbot I got similar advice, in a different form. As I have said, he was much engaged in the training of investigators (in this way he kept a close eye on the political movements in the whole of the kingdom), and, before my sudden departure (which I shall come to), I had become a senior trainee, directly under him. He took care to install the lesson that in any argument its premises must be given a great deal of attention and the greatest care must be taken not to jump into the delights of dialectics before those premises had been established. For this reason he made us, the trainees, confine ourselves to the facts, saying that he, and indeed many others, could produce the arguments, once the facts had been established. It was in trying to change the facts of one of my cases that my own misfortune occurred.

The Abbot had been asked by the King of France to establish the facts concerning an attack by the Duke of Alsace on the castle of Ain, which was subject to the Duke of Lorraine. It was winter when I and two others set off for Alsace, the roads broken and mirey, the nights very cold and snow lying in many places. And as we got nearer to the mountains the snow increased and our two weeks' journey became more and more uncomfortable. When we arrived at the castle of Ain we were in the worst of tempers, angry with our hosts and with each other, and being unexpected and arriving late, were given a rough and damp sleeping place that first night.

My companions were two high-born Frenchmen, of a kind common at Laon where political manoeuvring between students seemed almost to be encouraged, who looked down on students from outside France and made their lives difficult. In an effort to show my superiority, I there and then decided that we would stay only two nights, before returning, and somehow would fit all our work into those two days. My two colleagues made little argument against a short stay, seeing a chance to show up a non-Frenchman in a bad light and so I had my way. From this piece of senselessness flowed the rest of the story, because the investigation, from the reports we had, was seen to hinge on the matter of provocation, and although the key witnesses were not available to us, we proceeded to manufacture facts to fit our previously developed and quite fanciful theory, an approach quite contrary to the teachings and instructions of the abbot – and of course quite against my own father's customs.

A full description of the affair would be as unrewarding as a description of a shoddy building or the reading of a badly composed manuscript (of which many are produced, beautiful in appearance, but containing nothing of value). The report we gave to the abbot was so misleading that it was easy for his acute mind to see the absurdities. The interview that I then had with him was something that even now I remember with pain.

He put it to me that in heavy matters, involving great mental and physical stress, he thought I would always be inclined to look for short cuts and the easy answer. He said that this was a very normal fault in men and he quoted a saying that I have always remembered:

'To every complicated problem you will always find one simple easy answer – which will be wrong!'

He needed men for his work in the political field who would always reason well even when the mental and physical loads were severe. My work, he said, had become more and more unsatisfactory as he had made it more difficult and it was his judgement that I would be happier and more effective in work of a different kind and of a more routine nature.

I have not mentioned the religious training that we all received in the abbey, during the whole of our stay there. Some third of our time was spent in the Abbey Chapel, either taking part in the regular services or receiving instruction, as novices. As a special trainee of the abbot I was inclined to regard this religious training as time ill-spent, as an intrusion into my proper work, and yet I can still look back, and remember very clearly the peace I found in that ancient chapel.

16

(I know now that it is one of the biggest mistakes a man can make to struggle with a job for which he is not fitted in preference to a job which he can perform adequately and happily.)

The Abbot had everything prepared. He explained that my old mentor, the Archbishop of York, had been asking for one of his trainees for some time to fill a vacancy in this parish of Tentwell as a curate. At the time it was a growing parish, still recovering from the wasting it suffered when the first William made his mission of hate to the northern counties. It had a fair proportion of arable land, reasonably level and well drained. The population in those days was four hundred souls and a church was in the process of building to the west of Tentwell itself. It was the intention to appoint a vicar in a year or two, when the church was sufficiently finished to accommodate a small congregation. He was now instructing me to leave Laon straight away and to report to the Archbishop of York.

I was deeply shocked. The theological side of my Laon training had not prepared me for priesthood that in any case I regarded as a special vocation for those with a strong inclination to administer and preach the Christian religion. I could not feel that I had any such inclination or sense of vocation. For several minutes I could say nothing and Anselm, sensing my grief, carried a chair round the table and sat down next to me.

'My son,' he said, 'if I have a special talent, it is to form a reliable judgement of the way in which a man may most usefully spend his time, although sometimes the judgement is easy and sometimes hard. By far the hardest have been in the appointment of priests, those men by whom our church is judged by the people of any country. With those who have been inclined to follow book-keeping or law (so he described the future Treasurers and Chancellors of great estates!), the decisions have been easier, because I know that if they fail at one sort of task in their field another will soon be found for them, and in any case, people like that are usually checked, sooner rather than later, by their own kind.

'In the appointment of priests, however, I take the view that everything possible must be done at the start to avoid failure (I thought of my father's 'good foundation philosophy') because, with regard to the man himself, there is no one so completely beaten as a failed priest, and with regard to his parishioners several years of damage to them and in turn to the church itself might be done before he can be replaced.

'In your case I know that you have the ability to carry the teachings of the church to your parishioners and that you have also the courage and the knowledge and the heart to wrestle with all the low kinds of evil which you will meet with and to give fresh heart to those who are fighting for "righteousness' ".

He paused for a minute and then said with that wide, non-theological grin for which he was famous in the Abbey (and beyond), 'I can see that you have grown used to the idea while I have been talking and now understand the challenge better.'

Then to move my mind to other things and prevent unhealthy brooding, he added, 'Please say your goodbyes to your colleagues this evening and be prepared to start your journey to Calais and England at first light. You will have two companions, and as a cart and a mule must be sent back to our sister priory at Calais you will have the use of it for the first part of the journey.'

[Translator's Note: Being a little dismayed by the way in which failure for one project seemed to have barred our priest for ever from a wider life, and the way in which the Abbot had decided, peremptorily, that he would nevertheless be perfectly satisfactory in another job, I showed my translation to date to the Professor of Psychological Management Studies at the University of Toronto and asked him for his comments. His answer, very dryly, was to the effect that today's management practices had probably just about reached the Abbot's standards, over-promotion being the commonest cause of organisational failure and very difficult to deal with. The growth of sophisticated management selection processes inclined the organisation to blame everything but the man himself when things went wrong.]

My companions were travelling to Winchester, to the Royal Secretariat, where they were to be household clerks in King Henry's Treasury. Their talk was of taxes and the new form of geld surveys and when they tired of that they could go on for hours about the chances of promotion, who had to be cultivated and who could be ignored, and, in a word, all the senseless chatter of ambitious young men.

On the journey I was therefore left with much time to consider my own future and to wonder in particular about the reception I was likely to receive at Tentwell. I knew the village slightly, having delivered a bow to the squire there when I was twelve years old, journeying from my father's manor, twenty miles away, on an old pony which was regarded as mine. He had begged the bow from my father for a deer hunt with some royal personage who he wished to impress, but he lost it the next day when he was persuaded to give it as a 'present' to that same royal person. My father, when he heard, was angry, saying that he made bows as a hobby, for his own personal gifts, not for other people to give away.

The whole area in which Tentwell lies exists under that easy type of feudalism in which each man is measured and known for what he does for the community. In these small communities nothing is hidden and the problem of the squire with his taxes is as likely to be reviewed in the ale-house as often as the courtship of the youngest labourer.

As we travelled I wondered how I would be able to prove my own worth, having engaged to be a priest without any experience of the job. The people would be similar to those I had known on my father's estate and in the surrounding manors. To change their views or opinions was never easy and when talking to them you had to remember this, giving them time to consider and think. It was fatal to try to override them by fast talk and a welter of arguments. 'Hey-up, lad,' they would say, when as the son of the squire I tried to push them into untried situations or foist my boyish views, 'Hey-up lad, th'an gannin ower fast!' and, if I wanted to continue, I had no choice but to start again, at a slower pace.

It got me to thinking, on our journey, how much I owed to Anselm for my six years' tuition. He too had often said, 'Pause!' and in fact when he became philosophical during a tutorial he would sometimes talk to us about the 'pause element' and say that, depending on when and how a man pauses you might judge whether he was trying to arrive at the truth or only wagging his tongue. Few of my Yorkshiremen could ever be accused of 'wagging their tongues' – even ale seemed to make them slower! – and the 'pause factor' was clearly present in every conversation.

How would they accept me, a stripling clerk from a foreign abbey, as their apprentice priest, even though I had been bred in the area and my stock was well known? Would I ever be able to 'preach' – about the teachings of the church or anything else – to these stolid men with their well-formed views?

As we journeyed through the cold and wet countryside of first France and then England, with a rough crossing of La Manche in between, during which we all became very ill, I formed a rough plan of action for my forthcoming curacy, which after forty years I have not found it necessary to change.

My plan was in two parts.

First, I would work hard and systematically at those well-developed routines of the church which over many centuries had been seen to provide the religious needs of people, particularly at the critical times in their lives such as baptism, death and marriage. All the procedures and rituals were well documented and as I had a strong voice, with a good bearing heightened by that tallness common in my family, I felt I would have no difficulty in satisfying my parishioners in these matters.

It would be a strong persuasion, to both me and them, that the ecclesiastical court, to which they were all subject on a wide variety of matters, and which had, effectively, power of life and death, insisted on proper credentials from those appearing before it, those without credentials often being thrown into prison until their background could be established.

And with regard to sermons, which were starting to be expected, even from junior clergy, I had sat under some of the best sermonisers in Europe, at Laon, and I remembered much which would be useful at the start.

The second part of my plan concerned the mysticism of our religion, which I fully understood to be essential but which at that stage had not yet entered my experience. The nearest

I had come to it was in the Chapel of the Abbey of Laon where I had sometimes felt that great peace which does not seek the explanation that of course could never be forthcoming.

(It was shortly after I left that the Cathedral of Laon was burned down, all except the chapel which was untouched.)

So my second resolve was that I would finish building the church at Tentwell in such a manner that all its elements would carry that peace of God which I had found in Laon Chapel. As a formula for design, I do not recommend this to those who wish for an easy life. Advisors in such matters (they were many!) go for ornament and complexity, and how I achieved my objective of pure simplicity is for another place. Let me inform the reader, however, that only four weeks ago, as I write, the second Henry (for so I call the present King, who is bringing a welcome peace to our country), journeying south after his historic meeting with King Malcolm of the Scots, stepped aside, riding some twenty miles out of his way, to spend an hour in our church, his emissary saying that its reputation as a place of peaceful meditation had been mentioned to the King on a visit he had made to Laon earlier in the year. He asked to be alone in the church and I was told by the verger, who kept a discreet watch from the tower stairs, that he spent the time sitting quietly in a chair in the Squire's pew. The Verger could not tell whether he slept or not. Before he left however the King called me to him and graciously gave me ten marks for the poor of the parish.

Returning to my journey to Tentwell, I made two visits on my way. The first was to my father's house, where I had not been for eight years and I found him little changed. Our meeting, though cordial, was difficult in that we did not find much common ground in our recent experiences and his eagerness to get back to some experiments on different bow shapes was as keen as mine was to get to Tentwell. He seemed much relieved when I said that I would like to depart the next day.

My other visit was to York to be ordained by Archbishop Gerard, because although ordination would have been possible in Laon, I had asked for it to be done in my own country. I was the last to be ordained by Gerard who died shortly afterwards. Thomas the second followed him for five years and then we had that noble and holy man, Thurstan, for twenty-one notable years.

The ceremony was quickly performed, the archbishop being on the point of departure for Hereford, his old See, so that I was only a day in York as well and my journey to Tentwell was done with little delay. However the archbishop did ask me to call on my way at the village of Didsby, where the elderly vicar lived who had enjoyed a responsibility for Tentwell as one of his outlying parishes. When I arrived I found a man frail and weak and now quite unable to carry out his full duties in his several parishes. He was philosophical about it, explaining that while he spent all his waking time on the business of the church, he found it necessary to sleep more and more!

He was quite aware that matters were not right but said that he was devoting his time to making sure that each of his parishioners was properly accredited in the eyes of the church so that pastoral visits and church masses had often to be foregone. He was a good old man, highly thought of by his people, difficult to replace. He warned me that I would find some irregular marriages which would need to be put right and several rather elderly baptisms to be seen to. I did not see him again, for he died three months later.

So I came to Tentwell and while some parts of my life there will unfold as I tell Edwin's story, it is his story which I wish to concentrate on, and the reader must seek elsewhere (perhaps in the diocesan records) if he wishes to learn more about how Tentwell became a notable church and parish in which I managed to remain in tenure for the whole of my ordination – that in itself being a notable feat, requiring no little political manoeuvring!

CHAPTER TWO

Edwin Starts His Tale

Priest: This morning Edwin came to see me and it was too dull to write, even with candle, so I talked to him about the report. And now he has gone, with the light better, I will set down something about our talk.

I warned him that I intended to write as a scholar with the exactness which had been demanded of me long ago by that great and good man, the Abbot of Laon, and after considering this he said, 'For two years when I was young I was a scout for the Duke's army and was often brought before commanders for fierce questioning. I found out then how hard it is to be sure of what you have seen and not to mix in some of your own imaginings. You will need question me as did the Duke's commanders.' His face relaxed and he laughed, as though to say that my questioning could never be as close as theirs, but I believe I came very near for he was often tired at the end of our talks.

At the time I came to think about writing up Edwin's journey my spirits had been heavy for some time with the thought that ever since Laon I had done no task which had not been a poor compromise both with the truth and our Holy Faith itself. And so, hoping and believing that a long scholarly exercise would raise my spirits, I decided to give myself the task of writing up Edwin's journey in a form which would not only be exact but would be admired for its learning. I did not know whether to try to explain this to Edwin but what he said about his army training told me that there was no need to press the point much further. The exactness of his memory of things that happened eleven years ago I will check, as I have said, by careful questioning. Not only will this help us to arrive at the truth but also it will give me time to write down his story in my ancient code. So I asked him to remember the verse from Ecclesiasticus:

> 'Let thy speech be short, comprehending much in few words.'

A greater worry is that some of the events will only have been seen by others, and I stressed to him the need to tell me whenever an event had been one which he did not see himself but heard of from someone else. And I asked him to remember the Scriptures,

> 'God has chosen the foolish things of the world to confuse the wise',

so that we must be careful to avoid things (and men, and the sayings of such men) which are foolish, if we ourselves are to remain wise.

So this is his story, with some interruptions from me to get at the truth.

Edwin: Shortly after landing at Southampton I got a job as woodsman in the Royal Forest nearby.

Priest: How did you get the job? How did you manage this so soon after landing when you were still having trouble with your native tongue? (When he arrived at Tentwell his English was again as good as mine, although he frenchified some words as I do myself.)

Edwin: At the sheriff's office in Southampton I found an old comrade from the days when I made siege towers for the duke. His name was Daniel Roberts, and I gave him five pence to have a letter written to the forest office at Lyndhurst to say that the sheriff's office knew of me and recommended me for a woodsman's job. I remember that they thought little of the letter at Lyndhurst, the head clerk saying it was another 'five-penny chit', but they seemed to like the look of me and took me on, for a trial.

Priest: Wait! Hold there! You didn't come into England to work in a Royal Forest in Hampshire! Why were you going to all that trouble to get a job you didn't want?

Edwin: You are right, I was forgetting. When I talked to Daniel Roberts – we had a jug of ale in an ale-house by the side of the docks, (the rats were scrabbling in the under-thatch; we had to keep the jug covered with a platter. The place was filthy.) – I soon told him I had come to go back to my old village in Yorkshire and wanted to set off to walk up through the kingdom that very day if I could.

Daniel screwed his face and reached across to grasp my arm, saying fiercely, 'You are crazy! You can't know how bad these times are for travellers! No one would think of going on a trip alone today, even for a short spell!'

I had heard some things talked about in France but was still taken aback. 'Can people really not travel about anymore, then?' I asked.

'If you have to travel, do it in a big, well-armed group. With men you know and can trust. And steer clear of the main highways, where robbers are at work all over the kingdom.'

I sat back and thought. I knew no one, so that joining a travelling group of strangers might be more dangerous than travelling alone should I get with a group of rascals. 'Where can I find a group, who I can trust, who will be going in my direction?' Clearly I would have to work on this before I could start.

'I have heard,' he said, 'that groups gather at local inns, where travellers stay for a few nights until they find the right companions. It will be better to take time over this, you being just returned and having forgotten our ways. In your place, I should not try to set off soon at all but would wait until next year when things will be better and the strife might be finished.

'There is an inn near Lyndhurst,' he went on, 'and I know the chief forester for that section of the forest. He will be glad to help you.' 'Will he give me a job?' I asked. 'I have not too much money.'

After an hour or more further talk, I gave him five pence to get the chit written and signed by the sheriff so that I could journey through the forest, and then attached myself to a muleteer who said he would get me to Lyndhurst before nightfall.

I slept that night in the inn and the next day got a job in the New Forest as a forester.

Note by Priest: As I am familiar with work in the Royal Forests, having attended three or four eyres in the Forest of Galtres, once as a juror, I would like to give the reader a description of the work of a forester as a background to Edwin's story. So that Edwin can go on with his story, I have written this as an appendix to this report, where some of Edwin's experiences are also included.

Priest: Civil war was raging and everyone had to be suspicious of strangers. It was important to find out as much as you could about conditions before you started your long journey and I am wondering who you spoke to most about this.

Edwin: I worked with two men, and of course we spoke often. I also took a part-time waiter's job in the ale-house and had talk every evening with most of the travellers.

My mate in the forest was John, a steady and hard worker but not a talker. His favourite expression was 'Bugger 'em', changed sometimes to 'Bugger it', and occasionally 'Bugger 'ee', when it was directed at me. In giving me a job he might say, 'T'ride near Patsey Brook is to be done, bugger it,' or 'Deer am settled in Laskey Spinney, bugger 'em,' this last in a rising voice, in some pleasure. If I pressed him about his experiences, say of some local skirmishing of Stephen's troops or the Royal shoots, all he would say was, 'Them was soon gone, bugger 'em,' or, 'Ey frightened deer, bugger 'em,' so that I got nothing out of him. He had worked in the woods for more than twenty years and was content with his lot.

Priest: 'He was content, but the strict laws of the forest made his job very dangerous. The temptation, always present, to mistake the King's venison for his own might have lead to death or mutilation after a trial in the King's Court!

Edwin: The severe laws are set up to protect the gentle deer in these large wastelands. As you know, the cruel danger of the laws are well known to all the workers in the forest and John, who had thought on these matters for a long time, would sometimes say quietly to me, 'See nowt, lad, see nowt,' and by sticking to this rule of minding his own business he had avoided conflict in a place where even a witness to a deer-stealing was in great danger. We were not rangers but woodsmen and John's adage was a good one.

Priest: And your other companion in the forest?

Edwin: The other man I got to know well was my boss, Hugh, the forester in charge of the bailiwick, an experienced forester from a family of foresters. His father, Theo, who had also been a head forester, was the son of an Italian mercenary in the Conquerors' army. Hugh's brother was in charge of the Linwood bailiwick.

Besides John and me, Hugh had eight other men to keep his two-thousand-acre bailiwick in a state that would be satisfactory to the king on his once-a-year visit to hunt in the forest. And Hugh managed to get other work done by allowing agistment to local farmers in return for jobs done by them in the forest. The two new drainage ditches at the west end of the bailiwick had been dug by two farmers in return for agistment for nineteen cows and three horses. And, while I was there, a great oak which had fallen down in the middle of the bailiwick was cut up by the servants of the squire of Longton who were given in return one quarter of the thick timber.

When I first started work, Hugh would give out the work to John who he had known for many years and spare me only a glance, but, when he found I was prepared to work as hard as John, he opened up about the forest problems. I think he found me an easier audience than John.

Priest: I can see already that you must have got most of your information from the ale-house gossipers, men with new adventures and talk fresh from the road. But before we start on the gossip, I have always been interested in ale-houses, tell me about yours. How was it run?

Edwin: In my nine months in the forest I got to know it well and still think about it.

It was seven by forty paces (I paced each pace many times when serving beer!) with walls of wattle and mud except that at one end there was a boarded extension. It was quite high and at the extension end there was a big shelf or loft where visitors sometimes slept when the inn was full. There was only one door, alongside the bar, so that the barman, Martin, could check the comings and goings of his customers while preparing the food and drinks. In the centre of the floor, near the bar, was a narrow plank table about ten feet long, with benches.

The floor was made of thick wooden sets covered with rushes. Travellers often swore at the unevenness when they tripped in the half-light carrying loads to their sleeping places. Clean straw palliasses were provided for a halfpenny and these were put across the room, each side nearly meeting in the centre.

The evening meal – it was the same every night – consisted of a thick mutton stew poured over a thick slice of pea-flour bread, on a platter, and each guest was given two small jugs of ale. I can see it now, in the flickering light of five rushlights on the table, the travellers lying on their palliasses along the room, each surrounded by his bundles and packs.

Usually they were not either talkative or friendly. Sometimes one would know another traveller who was staying the same night, but usually all were strangers, and they would lie on their palliasses, silent, suspicious and watchful. It was easier later, after two jugs or more of beer, and it was only then that I had a chance of learning something about what was happening on the roads going north.

It was after I had been at the inn a few days that Martin asked me to help in the evenings, in return for ale and a meal, and I gladly set to, as a waiter during the meal and afterwards as a replenisher of tankards.

Some travellers carried only light loads, but others travelled with servants and mules, and their packs had to be brought in and stacked for safe-guard. As I have said, it was a sight to remember, when all were settled, to see some ten or twelve piles of packages, of every shape and size, often stacked quite high, and some without doubt very valuable. Outside was a small lean-to where animals could be tied and also a privy. Ten paces from the door a spring was covered over and flagged. The roof of the inn was straw-thatched and there was only one small window, near the cooking fire. On cold nights most of the customers drank their ale seated on benches near the large cooking fire.

Martin did not brew his own beer. He had no time to keep an inn and brew beer and his ale came from Ringwood, on a two-horse dray, twice a week.

I was very careful not to be seen to be asking questions. Since Stephen had stirred up the barons, informers were widely used by both sides so that there was a great wariness of questioners. Towards the end of the evening, when my serving duties were over, I would sit quietly with a glass of ale and listen to any talk, not saying much other than that I was a retired soldier, now a woodsman.

Travellers of many kinds came to the inn, usually for one night, on the way either from the north on the way to France, or on the return journey, or travelling between the West Country and London. From the north there often came wool traders and I can remember filling two traders from York with beer so that I could hear news of my own countryside.

Priest: During this time of very hard work in the forest and the inn were you making a lot of money? How were you paid?

Edwin: You should start another chapter and I will tell you how we arranged payment matters in the forest.

CHAPTER THREE

Living in the Forest (Edwin speaking)

When Hugh made me a woodsman he told me there would be no pay but that I would live well on 'what came with the job'. When I asked what it was that came with the job, he replied that it was easier to say what did not which was 'venison' in all its forms, but particularly every sort of deer and wild boar.

The forest laws of England and their cruel enforcement have been known throughout Christendom for a century or more so I saw no need for Hughy to repeat them, and yet after working in the forest I saw that the temptation to a woodsman would be so great that the laws needed to be repeated very often. Deer in the forest become used to the forest workers and the temptation to kill a hind that has become tame is very great, especially when a worker will know good hiding places in the forest for weapons and meat.

The word from Hughy was: 'Don't expect help if you're caught with venison,' to which he could have added, 'And to save my skin I shall press charges all the way.'

The many different jobs in the forest often produced things that we could sell outside. Most often we were left with piles of firewood which we could carry out ourselves or sell to one of the local donkey men. Carrying out the firewood on our backs was heavy work but the donkey men also gave us extra work because we had to go with them to the edge of the forest each time, in case they picked up extra wood on their way. Hughy took for himself two pence in the shilling for everything we got, and for good firewood we tried to get two pence for a back load and four pence for a donkey load.

When Hughy gave us our jobs he might say, 'Sorry men, it's a bad job, replanting seven score trees in Bootle Spinney. But next week we're back to trimming the lower branches in Nanton and there should be plenty of pickings.' The replanting would give us nothing except a few bundles of kindling but the trimming would give us some good thick firewood, or better still, some saleable building timber.

In fact little money changed hands, because even when we 'sold' the produce we were paid in kind, not only from our main customers, the three manors near the bailiwick and the monastery, but also from the cottagers who had to have firewood and were not allowed to cut it from the woods near their cottages. Our actual 'pay' varied, from foodstuffs of all kinds, in due season, to cloth pieces and clothes and occasionally the iron tools we needed in the forest.

Although barter was common, some money needed to change hands because those who held the manor from the crown had to send cash to the King's Treasury as rent. Thus, from time to time we were told to insist on money from our customers and it was difficult to get them to part with the little they had saved.

What was yielded by the forest in quantities of wood, trimmings and grazing had become fairly settled over many years and it was not hard for woodsmen to find reasonable livings as well as keeping the verderers and regarders content. A woodsman's knowledge of the forest in which he spends most daylight hours is so much greater than anybody else's that he can usually turn aside demands which might destroy the system.

Hugh had meetings every month with the verderers about the forest, its animals and his woodsmen. He never told us what happened at these meetings but I never saw anything decided which altered the way we worked in the forest. The warden of the forest was separate from the verderers and to him Hughy had to pay a yearly fee, in cash, so that the warden's fee to the Crown could be collected.

The Regarders were held by the Crown to have final responsibility for the forest and to answer to the Crown for its well-being. The Regarders were local knights who carried out a close inspection of the forest every three or four years. Everybody who worked in the forest had a sworn duty to guard against trespassers and anyone who might steal or damage anything, dead or alive, within it. The penalties for neglect were severe.

As I have said I lodged in a small inn on the edge of the forest and it was several weeks before I learned that it was owned by Hughy although he was not often there. It was to Martin at the inn that dues were paid for everything which Hughy sold himself from the forest, and I often saw Martin handing out tallies, in return for goods or cash, for such things as permission to hunt small animals, to collect plants and herbs, to sink eel traps in the Planey brook or to collect large timbers.

Each week the steward of the warden came to the inn with a two-wheeled cart drawn by an old bullock to collect the payments due to the warden. Hugh would bargain with this steward who would start by saying, 'What we have a right to expect each week at this season...' or perhaps, 'What we got this time last year...' Both Rampton, the steward, and Hughy had good memories and without any script could recall the outcome of each negotiation for some years back.

Priest: Tell me about one customer for your firewood who you dealt with yourself and tell me how he paid for it. How did you get it to him? What kind of wood did he like? What did he use it for in the main? Had he no wood of his own?

Edwin: These questions of yours bring back all the wranglings and quarrellings that went on about the forest products and the way we were paid for them. I recall very readily a customer called Walter of Donne who had a small farm of half a hide on the edge of the forest.

Walter kept twenty cows, a bull, a few swine, and some fowls. He grew mostly cabbages and barley. He had three children, two of them old enough to do some proper work on the farm. The bull was a small red one. His rent had to be paid in cheeses. He should have needed little from outside but in fact he had no fuel for heating and cooking, because, some

32

ten years before, the regarders had obtained an order which forbade him to cut wood on his farm for fifteen years because they said the property had an appearance of 'waste', an appearance forbidden by the King.

The regarders, usually unpropertied knights, perhaps experienced in war but nothing else, were always prepared to be knowledgeable about the appearance of the forest. As the general rule was that it, and also any neighbouring properties, should appear 'wild' and 'untouched', conflict with those who owned neighbouring properties was continuous.

It was a pleasant day in October when I visited Walter on Hugh's behalf to settle the payment for the winter's supply of faggots. We sat in front of his stone fireplace, the door being open at our backs, His wife Maud, after bringing us some home-brew, settled down at her broadloom in the corner. We finished three jugs of ale while we argued about the quantity, the size, the weight, the ties, the mix of small and large sticks, and the extra cost due to main rides being blocked.

When we had settled, very roughly, about what he had had – we agreed it was very similar to last year, perhaps a little more – we had to decide what would be reasonable payment in terms of cheeses, or if cheeses could not be found, their value in terms of cabbages and barley, or even bacon. And we had to take in the value of three ditches that Walter had dug for Hugh in March on a joint boundary.

Walter had been taught (by a butcher uncle in Winchester) the new trick of placing a monetary value on all goods in an exchange, 'just to check' he would say, and at the end of our argument, after he had pondered for a little time, he said, 'That's nearly three marks the regarders have got out of me for the King.'

For myself, I knew that after the 'payments' had been through Hugh's hands there would be a hunk of bacon for me and probably a small cheese which I could use for my midday meals in the forest.

Priest: How were the faggots carried from out of the forest to Walter's place?

Edwin: He had a donkey with a pack harness and his ten-year-old son spent nearly a week carrying the faggots from

Bent Coppice, one and a half miles away. The poor donkey was loaded with five faggots each journey, two either side and one across the top, and sometimes the lad would carry one himself, if he was fresh.

Two weeks after our talk I was in Ringwood market and saw Walter's cheeses on a market stall carrying his blue mark, shaped like a crescent. In this way were the sticks I cut in the forest turned into money for the King, providing me and many others with a living on the way.

I had been sent to talk to Walter about payments because my stump was inflamed, making it difficult to use my hook on forestry work. Any bargaining I did was fairly useless because both Hugh and Walter knew to a fraction how the settlement would finish up but Walter felt he owed it to his family to put up some kind of fight. His wife who had a reputation for 'keenness' listened to our talk, and, while she said little, her movements and coughs told Walter clearly what she thought about her good viands being sent to the warden – all because they were not allowed to use their own wood!

Part of my job this time was to warn Walter that next time half the payment would have to be in coin and they became more angry at this than at any insistence on a slightly lower value for cabbages or cheeses. Where thy would get this coin from was not clear to any of us but the King had to have coin for such things as paying his mercenaries, who could not be paid with cheeses or sides of bacon.

Walter and his wife, like everybody else, managed their lives without using coin, which they saw as a way, thought up by others of tapping into their private lives. Although feelings about coin were very different in the towns, the countryman had spent his whole life in barter – perhaps for his own labour, in return for goods, or in the exchange of all kinds of goods and produce for other kinds, or in getting some grazing in return for corn, or in lending a horse in return for the loan of a cart.

(Note by Priest: A few remarks by me on coins and the country people are given in Appendix Two)

Priest: Thank you for your stories of the forest. It must have made an interesting change after soldiering. Now tell me what you learned about the possibility of walking safely through the whole length of the country to get to your old home in Yorkshire. With a civil war raging and having been away for thirty years, what persuaded you that the journey was possible?

Edwin: I was persuaded by two things. The first was that life in the New Forest had shown me that a lot of England was unchanged by the war, and that the rule of law still held and, according to Hughy, was getting stronger. King Stephen himself had a reputation as a strengthener of laws.

So things were not nearly as bad and dangerous as Dennis, who was always a very cautious man even as a soldier, had told me.

The other thing that persuaded me was the regular coming and going of travellers at the inn, nearly all of whom had valuable loads which they had carried safely through the kingdom.

However, before I set off I would do two things.

First, I would not travel alone. I had seen that travellers journeyed almost always in small parties, usually strangers to each other but good enough companions on the road. This gave them protection against solitary robbers and made them more acceptable to local people who were generally suspicious of solitaries. So I would try to pick some good companions for the journey.

Then I would travel with a donkey. I had made a little money in the forest and still had most of the Duke's gift so it was an easy matter to buy a good little donkey when the time came to start. From a dealer in Ringwood I got a strong gelding called Jack, complete with harness, and until we were parted we worked well together.

Travelling time started in April, which would be nine months after I had joined Hughy, and I told him at Christmas time that I would have to leave him then to start my journey to the north.

CHAPTER FOUR

A Trip with Mad Dash Jack

In the inn I had heard them talk about a famous train of pack-horses from York known countrywide as 'the Mad Dash' and which came to the inn once or twice a year. One evening when I had been there a month I was helping Martin in the kitchen when we heard the sloshing and jangling and shouting and snorting of a large pack-horse train coming along the path out of the forest. Martin looked at me and said, 'Might be Mad Dash,' and ran outside. I followed quickly.

With other pack-trains which had come to the inn, the men on arrival straight away ran into the inn for beer, or to get the best places, or to talk to Martin, but I noticed that with the Mad Dash all had to be checked before anyone came in.

The train-master was known everywhere as Mad Jack. In that train he had ten horses and after they had pulled up I watched with interest as he went over each weary horse, checking the load and the gear, before letting them be offloaded, watered at the brook, then led to a tethering place and fed. Martin said, 'If Jack finds anything missing, even a little thing, he will send someone back for it, and will stay up himself until he returns.'

I found that Jack had a sheep farm in one of the Yorkshire Dales, passed on to him by his father, but as well as sheep he bred and trained pack-horses. He had regular runs from York to other towns with wool, cheeses or uncured sheepskins and

he came to Southampton twice a year with uncured skins. When he went back to York from Southampton he was partly loaded with French brandy and sometimes silk.

The skins he brought to Southampton were for the vellum factory at Winchester, the royal scriptorium being very careful about the kind of vellum they used, and having for many years carried out the final finishing in their own factory. They believed that skins from the small Dales sheep made the thinnest and best vellum.

Jack loaded up his train before each journey at a large pack-horse inn that was owned by the Archbishop of York and situated at the back of the cathedral. Loads were brought to him there from all over the Dales.

On arrival at our inn he offloaded onto pack-horses sent from Winchester. His Bill of Lading for the whole train was made out, as the horses were loaded, by a clerk from the Cathedral of York, and the goods were checked off on arrival by another clerk sent from the Winchester scriptorium who also checked on the French goods which were going to York. Jack never stopped to load or offload between York and his destination, saying that there were other men with other horses who could do the shorter journeys better but his job was to carry loads as fast as possible between distant towns.

Jack was a lean middle aged man with sharp features and he was always on the move when he wasn't asleep. The many different jobs which come up in a train had taught him the need to be always busy, whether checking the horses or the equipment, or the dryness and safety of the storage, or in finding food for the horses and men, or in instructing his men, or in actually working on such things as the tethers himself.

He regarded proper tethering as so important that he walked round with a tether mallet in his hand all the time he was at the inn. It was a heavy weapon, brass bound.

He had six men with him, four horsemen and two spearmen, but they said he took more men on other journeys when the goods he carried were more valuable. He said that the journey to London with Wensleydale cheeses was the most risky, the robber gangs being very active near London. His men were sons of neighbouring farmers in the Dales.

It was early winter when I saw Jack this first time and I saw a chance to have good and safe company all the way to York with this small band of armed and experienced travellers.

I asked Martin the next morning (Jack and his train were staying for three nights, to rest the horses and men) to talk to Jack about letting me go back with him to York, and Jack's reply was that he might think about it on his next visit but that this time he wanted to get back very quickly, without hindrances, because of the illness of his wife. As he was expecting to make his next trip to Southampton in March, I had to be content with this half-promise if I wanted to travel with him, and so reconciled myself to the winter in what turned out to be a very wet forest.

However Jack did arrive at the end of March, as promised, and I was all prepared. My little donkey had been bought and my pact with Hugh Torens was at an end. When Jack had had his meal and was settled down, I brought him another jug of ale and said that I was all ready to go with him back to York. Of course he had forgotten and was not pleased to be reminded.

'How much baggage?' he asked, and when I told him, at the same time mentioning the donkey, he became angry.

'A donkey is no good, how can he keep up with my fine horses?' He thought for a minute and then said, 'You will slow us down.'

In the end he said he would take me, but only if I agreed to drop out if I slowed him down.

The morning that we set off on our journey north everybody was up and about well before daybreak. Torches had been set up outside the inn and each horse was led forward in turn to be harnessed and loaded. The monk from Winchester was there and he checked each load most carefully before the horse was taken away to a temporary tether awaiting the signal to move off.

As day was breaking so that we could see the track into the forest Jack led off the first horse with two more in tandem behind. The next three lots of horses went in twos, with a driver to each pair, and the remaining horse, carrying the men's gear, was led by the last driver.

I, with my little donkey, trailed behind.

The speed of the horse train was something I had not prepared myself for. Horse trains in the army doddle along at a speed that suits the corporal in charge and as he is usually very elderly the speed is mostly a very slow walk. The Mad Dash train went all the time so fast that the drivers were running alongside their lead horses, getting some help from a rope tied to the pack-saddle.

They stopped for half an hour twice in the morning and twice in the afternoon. At noon they rested for an hour. So on a normal day, off at dawn and arriving at their inn early evening, they would be running for about nine hours. Allowing for bad places in the roads, and obstructions from trees and falls, they would normally do thirty to forty miles in the day.

After the first day's run, when I had fallen behind by more than a mile, I knew that I and my little donkey would never be able to keep up and that if they were to wait for us their speed would be halved. That first night when he had settled everything in at the inn and was resting on his palliasse I approached Jack.

'You did well, soldier,' he said. 'Not many can keep up with Mad Dash.'

'But I didn't keep up,' I replied, 'and I am very worn. I shall have to drop out.'

He ruminated for a little time and then said, 'If you are sure about that you will need to take a safer road than the one we are going to take. We go fast and have arms; few small bands can catch us or fight us, but the way we are going is dangerous for a solitary traveller. There is a safer track to the east. My driver, Hughy of Skipton, knows the road well and if you like I will ask him to guide you to the other road so that you will have a safer journey. Hughy will then leave you and come back to us on this road further north; he is the best runner of us all! And soldier, let me tell you, I do not want to see a fellow Yorkshireman get into trouble!'

Note Number One by Translator

There are three gaps in Father Riveaux' account, the first of these being the period between Edwin leaving the Mad Dash and then being found benighted in a hovel near Crendon on the Buckinghamshire and Oxfordshire boundary. Here we find that he has suffered a change in his fortunes, having started with money, a donkey and a guide, he is now skulking in a small hovel with no donkey and few possessions.

The reason for each of these gaps is that the sheepskins which should have told us all about these days had been badly cured and most of the ink had become illegible, and while I was tempted to write a story round the surviving fragments I decided finally that this would involve too much of my own imaginings.

We must conclude that in this Mad Dash – Crendon period, Edwin suddenly found the journey very different from the orderly series of inn-stops that he had planned all the way to Yorkshire. Possibly an attack of some kind had robbed him of his possessions and parted him from his donkey. However, his later thoughts while in the hovel at Thame reveal that he felt himself fortunate not to have encountered any of the 'bands' which were roaming the country, so we can only imagine other possibilities such as Edwin becoming separated from his guide when he had to chase after his donkey which had run off with all his baggage (and which of course he did not catch), or perhaps because the donkey had died.

The second gap is covered by a note later in the book.

CHAPTER FIVE

Edwin in Great Danger Near Oxford

I was in a hovel in a small hamlet between Thame and Aylesbury and from a deep sleep was shaken awake by the woman who said, 'The raiders are back, does tha' want to be found?'

'Soldiers?' I asked, half-awake.

'Murdering rascals, better to hide. They took our cows and goats a week ago.'

'Where is a place?'

'A path, hard to see, over the marsh into the wood. Our great Holy Lime comes first – the path goes straight to it. Plenty places, back of the tree.'

I grabbed my little pack and short sword, and was pulled across the road to a little path, hard to see in the dim light. She pushed me between some bushes onto it, hissing, 'Keep low and run fast, the path goes right first and then left of the Holy Tree.'

I ran in a crouch. The path was hard to find in the half-light and once I slipped off it into the black slimy bog. The lime tree was a couple of hundred paces, and, once behind it, I dropped onto the ground and got my breath back before standing up to look round it at the road and the hamlet. It was becoming light quickly and as I peered round the side of the huge tree I could see a loose column of about fifty men strung out along the road with the first men just coming to the first hovel.

I was standing in the deep litter that lay between the big roots of the tree and because it was a very magic tree it had many things in its cracks and crevices put there by villagers and travellers as gifts or thank-offerings to its mighty spirit. I even saw the glint of silver, a precious coin but well protected, even in those desperate times, by the tree's great magic.

I watched the band move slowly into the village. Some staggered. One fell, and would have been left, if a tall man at the end of the column had not turned back and helped him up, and something about the tall man seemed familiar. Many kept looking back as men will who are being chased. In the middle of the column, two were on tired horses that limped and stumbled. I could see only two long spears and no swords; most had heavy sticks or cudgels, using them to walk with.

They sensed some danger in the wood and one or two heads turned as they went past, but, as the woman had said, the track through the wet ground was not easy to see, and after a slow glance they passed on.

Outside the first hovel they found a cooking fire and it was only the work of moments for several to seize the brands and whirl them round their heads. Then a devilment took them and put new life into them and they ran to each hovel and set light to it, not caring whether people were inside or not. Everything was very dry after a time without rain and it was easy to fire the thatch and the wattles. Within minutes the whole hamlet was ablaze and there was no one to resist. Just two very old men and some women who ran with their children into the fields, the villains not bothering to follow.

Then the band, fearful that too much time had been lost, and that they had shown their position with the smoke from the burning village, hurried on down the road, and I went down the swamp path to the village and met the people coming back to their wrecked homes.

Although I had walked for five days since setting out from the New Forest inn, in a time of cruel civil war and general strife, I had, by the Goodness of God, escaped the attention of any of the bands which were roaming the country, this being the first time I had felt myself to be in any such danger.

There had been much talk in the inn about robber and other bands and I had become used to hearing about the different kinds.

Sometimes a band would be a local group going to join its army, and it would be cheerful, fully armed and well-led. But more often it would be a small, discontented mob, taking advantage of the general confusion to rob and kill.

In truth, the old days of Edward were far away, when, as my father used to tell me,

'A mother with a babe in arms could walk safely across all England.'

The larger military groups moved along the main roads, unafraid, sometimes giving tallies for food but more often just grabbing anything they wanted.

'For my two fat geese I got a little piece of birchwood with cuts in it!' one bent old wife told me, early in my journey, after we had followed such a group a day behind. And she showed me a crude tally that she would never be able to exchange for anything.

No matter how well-led an army band might be, no one seemed to be safe from it, not even when it was honestly led, but it was not hard to dodge this kind because of the noise they made. Twice I went into hiding as they passed, but I was frightened of meeting the better ones that had advance scouts, riding fast, holding people for questioning, on the lookout for recruits and money.

In the village, now nearly burnt out, some of the women had hidden near enough to the road to hear the villains talking and it seemed that they were running away after a skirmish and in an ugly mood. Bands like this one, of routed soldiers with some weapons, were very dangerous, often without leaders and frightened, angry, tired and hungry. They would harry everybody and make trouble in a savage and senseless way. This band had just been beaten by a company of Maud's own mercenaries.

'There goes all I had,' said my hovel woman, as she stirred the embers.

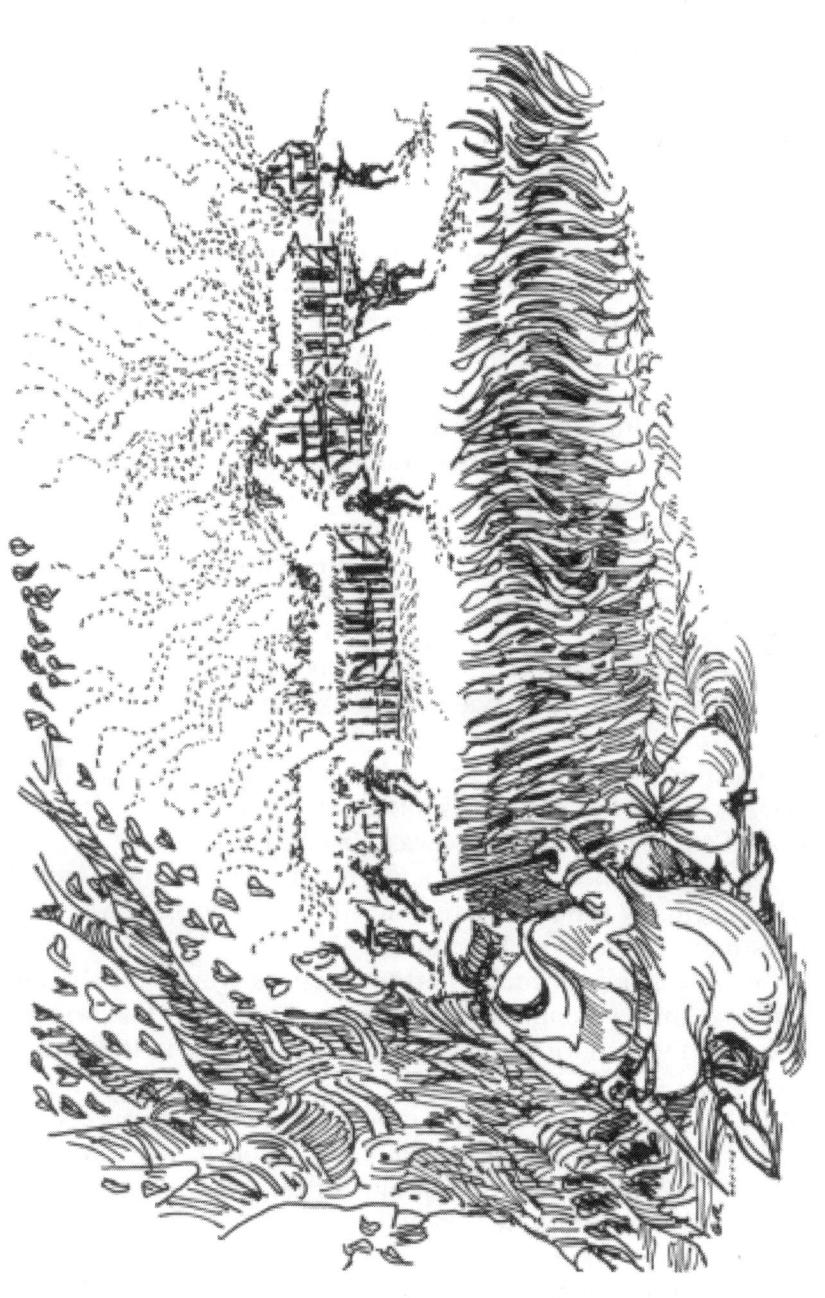

'What about the animals?' I said, having seen none. 'All gone,' someone answered, 'Driven away by the same villains on their way up.'

'They whipped my old cow along in front,' said my hovel woman. 'Shouted to me that that was easier than carrying the meat!'

I asked what they would do now and they said they were going to the Manor House at Crendon, to seek help from their lord. And they set off straight away – there was little to carry except two babies – and so I walked with them.

After about an hour we came to a well-built stone house and some farm buildings on a little hill and someone told us to go into an empty barn and doss down for an hour or two.

At noon on that fine May morning I went to the door and looked out, thinking about defence, sensing real danger.

As I stood, two men with dark blue capes came across from the Manor House and asked who I was. They were the lord and his eldest son. My hovel woman came out while we were speaking and to my surprise both men spoke to her warmly, the younger holding her hand. Other villagers then came out of the barn and I could see that the two men were well regarded by the village people. The lord was a slightly built man, thoughtful and slow of speech who walked with the help of his son's arm.

'He hurt his back at the taking of Jerusalem,' whispered my hovel women. 'He couldn't walk at all for three years. His son is deaf and has no speech; I was his nanny.'

The lord looked round us squarely, angrily, as a leader will who has many times used men for the cruel deeds of war. His eyes measured and commanded.

'We are going to make better defences, very quickly,' he said, 'so that we can be safe from such villains. You will all help and I will share with you what food we have in the Manor House.'

He had at the Manor House only five old or crippled men and twelve women, the rest having gone off to the wars. We were, all told, thirty-two, eight men of varying age and fitness, twenty women and four very young children.

'From somewhere I have to find an engineer-foreman,' he said, and after a little talk and questioning I found myself with

46

the job of fortifying an old manor house, very quickly, with a dozen men and a similar number of women.

We all saw that the main thing, and the only thing we would have time for anyway, was a stockade round the whole site. We had no way of making any defence which would hold against a regiment of proper soldiers for more than an hour but small bands of scoundrels, our chief danger, would not want to stay around, so that we might hold them until they changed their minds and wandered off.

We made a plan where we stood, in the barn doorway, with all the villagers looking on, drawing in the dust on the ground. A small wood, half a mile away would provide the posts. The lord had been going to make a deer forest when the trees were bigger and it took him ten minutes to decide to cut it down but such are the wastages of war, as of course he well knew.

We argued for over an hour about sizes, both the size of the area to be enclosed and the height of the fence. A large area would have allowed animals to be brought inside and perhaps some things grown, but a long fence would have been hard to build and difficult to defend. In the end we settled for a line of fence which would leave about thirty yards clear all round between it and the house so that bowmen in the house could cover the fence. The stockade was to be seven feet high, with three feet buried, so that we needed a great many ten-foot logs from the forest.

We gave ourselves two weeks to have it finished but I pressed for ten more men, not knowing where they would come from. The lord said he would go to his neighbour and borrow men but that we must help in turn with a stockade round the neighbour's house. He set off with his son, on horseback, within ten minutes, shouting to me to take charge and have the line of the stockade marked out before his return.

It took us four weeks. After five days we had to stop to fight off a small band of ruffians who came at us just before dusk. They had cudgels and sticks but no other weapons and seeing us drawn up in front of the manor, with four bowmen in front, they only shouted and shook their sticks before backing off. We stood guard all night and the next day we could do nothing as the band were camped about half a mile away. After another night they were gone and we started again. We were not attacked again before the fence was finished.

The 'bowmen' consisted of the elderly and greasy kitchen scullion, a goatherd long past any martial activity, a tall woman from the household, dressed in a man's cloak, and the lord's son, a good bowman, the only one we had! The bows we had found in the great hall where they had hung for many years. One broke as we tried to string it but the others were sound. The little squad of 'bowmen' looked very imposing, standing in a line outside the door of the manor. After a week, we got two elderly, ex-bowmen, from a neighbour so that the group had a good backbone of three capable archers. Sufficient, with the fence, to hold the manor – or so I thought.

When the attack finally came I was on guard, but asleep, stretched out on a step inside the fence that we had built to let the sentry look over the fence. The thing which woke me was the fence shaking, a shaking which didn't stop but which went on and on. As I opened my eyes I saw it was early dawn, with the sky just lightening. I had been weary after weeks of hard work as I took my post inside the fence about midnight and was quite unable to stop myself lying down on the step for a few minutes. And I had gone instantly to sleep, a sleep so deep that the fence must have been shaking for some time before I awoke.

As I opened my eyes, I found myself looking at a crude ladder, some thirty yards along the fence, with men jumping down it. It was their jumping on the ladder which was shaking the fence. They must have had another ladder outside the fence.

I had not been seen. I hid my face in my cloak and lay still.

As the fence stopped shaking, there was the noise of many men running to the Manor House and I looked up as they reached the door.

And my plan worked. The plan agreed with the lord during many talks while we made the fence. We were both practical soldiers and could each remember many ways those we fought had been made to enter traps of our making.

The attraction of a Manor House with a wide open door was a trap they had not been able to resist, particularly as we had left two barrels of ale on a table inside the porch, with a lamp to show them the way.

As the last man hurled himself thoughtlessly through the door I slammed the door shut by a rope in my hand which dropped a heavy stone and drove home a heavy iron bolt, closing the door firmly.

We had taken all the people out of the house and bolted the windows from the outside.

We had the villains like rats in a trap.

All soldiers who have fought their way through killing battles will know something not only about the feints and ruses, snares and enticements, which are commonly used but also about the grander tricks which are used by his general

The Old Duke used to say, 'The best soldier is brave and full of tricks.' And he himself was a legend both for bravery and for the way he could deceive his enemy. In fact tricks often need that kind of bravery, perhaps the most difficult kind, which involves being quite still in the face of attack.

Guard duty on a castle wall is not a way to learn soldiers' tricks, but battle, and the fear of death, make a man learn, very fast, those tricks which can be used to overcome an enemy and so save his own life and the lives of his comrades. He must also have a good understanding of all the tricks that an enemy might try against him.

Bravery requires steady determination and a fixed purpose, nearly always, while tricks require imagination and talent and, quite often, the need to 'reculer pour mieux sauter'. But I have often seen too that he who is not brave will commonly think of tricks as a way to avoid the need to be brave.

Perhaps the greatest ruse of all is to trick an enemy into moving into a weak position, either before or during a battle. As everybody knows, King William beat King Harold at Senlac because he feigned a retreat and tricked the English out of a position which was very strong, and from which they had held off the French for half a day. And this feigned retreat would not have worked if William had only planned to halt his retreating men after a time and turn the retreat into a counterattack because troops in retreat after a hard battle are not easily turned. But William closed the trap by a cavalry attack on the flank of the English, so that, just as in sword fighting, an opponent is most open with his sword raised high for a killing stroke, William's victory was gained by a surprise onslaught on the English at the very moment when they believed themselves to be the victors.

Nearly all good tricks work by coaxing an enemy to move into a trap, and this is done by making the way into the trap seem easier or less dangerous than other ways, or one which will somehow give him superiority. And if the trick is to succeed, he must be well into the trap, quite unable to retreat, before he discovers his mistake. At Senlac, the English house-carls were too far down the slope of the hill before the cavalry charged into their flanks to have time to retreat into their old positions.

As with a baited trap for animals, the bait in a military trap must be well chosen and be of a kind which will seem desirable even to a suspicious and cautious enemy.

The bait at Senlac were the backs of the French foot-soldiers as they pretended to flee. This after a day of cruel fighting being a sight so welcome to the English that they could not hold back.

But military mischiefs do not always require a bait. For example if an enemy seems certain to take some particular direction, mischiefs can be arranged in advance, the use of ambuscades on a marching column being one of the oldest military tricks. Perhaps however it might be said that the bait is really there, but invisible, being the sight of a clear road ahead with no signs of an enemy!

Crueller mischiefs, such as poisoning wells and burning crops, can rebound, should the tide of battle change. But some would regard them not as tricks but as much a part of war as the sharpening of spears or the taking of plunder.

Priest: Your tales of mischiefs and deceits cover ground which, you might not be surprised to hear, a parish priest comes across frequently, though not with quite the cruelty and slaughter met with by a soldier. I have at least three parishioners who regularly try to trap me into saying that their personal conduct is perfectly satisfactory in the eyes of God, and the bait they put out has included geese at Christmas and a whole cheese on Lady day.

While I'm always eager to listen to your reminiscences will you please tell me how this is connected with the attack on your lightly fortified house by the villains of the forest?

Edwin: I wanted to show you that soldiering is not only about sticking your sword in another man in face to face fighting but also about deceiving and confusing a foeman by a multitude of tricks so that when face to face fighting has to be done the task will be easier and victory more certain. With the best tricks, face to face fighting never appears, although victory is certain. My trick with the manor house was the kind of trick which gave us victory without fighting.

Note Number Two

The next two sheets of vellum were badly mildewed so that we have to guess what happened to Edwin between his trapping the villains in the farmhouse and reappearing in the hinterland of Lincolnshire.

We can easily guess that the villains would be given short shrift by the lord of the manor and his angry villagers who had just been burned out of their homes. And that after that Edwin would plead that he had to be on his way.

He would depart with the thanks of everyone and with all the best advice he could get about the state of the country between Oxfordshire and Yorkshire.

The advice would certainly include a strong warning to go east, away from the south-west from where bands of armed men were starting to ravage towns in the rest of the midlands.

And he would be warned to keep away from Yorkshire for a while as news of King David's invasion would just have reached them and they would have no means of knowing how far the Scottish King would march through Yorkshire into England.

The Lincolnshire Wolds might seem to be a good place to make for, being away from the main roads through the country and having one or two little ports where he could if necessary take a boat back to France. He could stay there if necessary until the position of the invading army and the southern rebellion became clearer. So we next find him walking quietly along a road in central Lincolnshire wondering where he was going to sleep that night.

Note by the Bishop of Lincoln, Found with Ancient Document

The following Note, by the Bishop of Lincoln, was at the bottom of the bundle of vellum scraps. It was written in a fine hand, by a professional scribe, and refers to the windmill saga described in the next chapter.

We cannot guess how it came into Father Riveaux's keeping. Possibly the Bishop of Lincoln was an old friend from Laon days and called to see him, perhaps after a Bishop's Assembly at York. In talking, Riveaux might have mentioned his talks with Edwin and Lincoln might have said, 'I know all about windmills, even wrote a note on one which we built in Louth, perhaps the same one. I will send you the note for interest.'

The idea came as we walked back from Matins, last Monday.

I have been Bishop of Lincoln for five years and have taught myself to think about the problems of my people at times when not engaged in the Heavenly Offices to which I am directed by my consecration. I find that I meditate on practical matters best when I walk, and in the ten minutes it takes to walk from the abbey to my house I have solved many problems.

Canterbury is an old friend, we were together in Laon and for a time were fellow students at Winchester. His personal letters are friendly and give me much encouragement but whenever I get a letter from his chief scribe, officially sealed and carried by his own rider, I know that it will be something more serious.

And so the letter that his rider brought last week proved to be. Without preamble or explanation it ordered me to take a personal interest in the new wind machines which are now being made to grind corn, and he asked me to make sure that one machine at least would be erected and in use in Lincoln before next harvest.

Now, as is well-known by Canterbury himself as well as my own people I myself happen to have no understanding of mechanical matters or in fact of most practical matters, being by training and inclination an intellectual and a lover of precision, accuracy and the finer things of life. In fact the fumbling practices of artisans as they go about their work is repulsive to my training and upbringing.

Only last week my mare Phoebe cast a shoe in the village of Ardham and as she is the only horse I will ride I waited with my small party outside the blacksmith's shop for her to be re-shod. Once again I had a chance to watch how such a place worked and once again I recognised a likeness to the way in which beasts and birds build their hides and nests. There was no discussion, intelligent or otherwise, just a few grunts and gestures as the work was passed from the fire to the anvil and back again and the shoe finally fitted and nailed onto the mare's hoof. It was as though the work was done by instinct, without pleasure, not by free men but by people driven by their trade, and I have seen the same thing with masons, wheelwrights, carpenters and farmers.

And it has taken me three days to work out that the reason why Canterbury has ordered me to be the master mechanic of wind machines is because he intends wind machines to be used in a highly political matter of which every aspect must be intellectually mastered. I believe he intends to use wind machines as a way of giving the Holy Church a tighter hold on the people through a church law which will forbid the hand-milling of corn in houses and farms, and rule that all milling will be done by wind machines which will be owned by the church!

And this ambitious plan will only work if the wind machines really work and produce flour as good or better than that produced by hand-grinding methods. Hence the need for a first-class intellectual approach to the manufacture and operation of wind machines which had resulted in his letter to me.

I had no complaint with the politics. Our people had been badly unsettled by the Civil War and were giving less attention to their devotions and practices than we deem to be necessary. Some ancient practices such as were practised in pre-Columbian times were being whispered about as a better way to survive the dangers of the times and it was becoming difficult for the Christian Church to stay close to its people. A law that insisted on the bulk of the people's food passing through its hands could only bring the church nearer to its people.

As I walked along I remembered a sentence from Marcus Aureleus; 'Give thyself time to learn something new and good, and ceased to be whirled around.' The last part of the quotation and the subject of windmills had a connection which I found humorous, so that I laughed aloud to the astonishment of my two companions.

I had collected around me in Lincoln people similar in inclination to myself and the two who were with me at that moment were the Master of the Scriptorium and the Treasurer of the Diocese. Both had great power because of their knowledge and we three made a strong team that headed the administration.

Back in my room I looked up the quotation from Marcus and found that it was followed by, 'But then thou must also avoid being carried about the other way. For those too are triflers who have wearied themselves in life by their activity, and yet have no object to which to direct every movement, and, in a word, all their thoughts.'

Marcus seemed to be saying that a balance had to be struck between the routine work which always had to be done dutifully and new work which would provide stimulation and new activities.

I knew that there lived in the village of Dunstan an elderly man who had built himself a stone house of elegant appearance some ten years ago on land that had been bought for him by King Henry. I had never enquired too much about his circumstances – King's favourites are better left alone – but it came back to me that he had been an engineer in the King's employ and that his son was now a highly regarded engineer at the King's court.

It occurred to me that he might be able to help with this windmill business and I sent to ask him to come and see me. He did not hurry and it was five days before he appeared outside my dwelling on an old mule.

Although I knew him to be about seventy years old, when he entered I was surprised to see an active upright man whose bright eyes regarded me suspiciously. He was obviously at home in the company of men of quality.

I immediately told him of my problem with the windmill and even confessed that I was undecided on how to proceed, not being a practical man and having senior colleagues who also were more religious than practical.

He did not interrupt me and when I finished he sat for a moment or two and then gave me a lecture that I have always remembered.

'However clever we are,' he said, 'you and I and our colleagues, we must always remember that, when it comes to making things, someone, at the end, has to put his hands to work on wood or iron or stone and shape it or build it so that it will serve some purpose we have envisaged.

'And when that person comes to use his hands, they should be controlled both by his own brain and by ours. If they are controlled entirely by his own brain, he himself will have to decide many things, such as the size and strength of the parts, and this he might not be mentally furnished to do.

'Think how many cathedrals, and even houses, have fallen down, even before they were finished, when the building of them was left entirely to stone-masons.

'And if we ourselves, having the necessary mental furnishings, and wishing a proper measure of control to come from our own brains, we will have to use a way of communicating our ideas to him.

'But remember that the men we are talking about cannot usually write or read and that their mathematical powers are negligible, so that the language we would like to use, which will usually be the language of mathematics, will be too difficult for them. We must therefore use another other language, which I will call the language of the engineer.

'An important component of this language is the system of having something copied which already exists, that is to say pointing the workman to an already existing pattern of what is required.

'To the non-engineer this might seem a simple and trouble-free way of obtaining say a house or a cart or even a siege machine.

'But you must be careful, because in fact it might be unwise to try to copy that particular article exactly. For instance if it was made some time ago the exact materials might be impossible to obtain. With stone, the quarry might have closed, or with wood-seasoned timber that type might not be instantly available. So before the simple order is given, 'Copy that article,' at least some effort must be made to find out whether the same materials are to hand. If not, the design might have to be changed.

'A better system is to pass all important requests through the hands of the pattern-making individual or section, who over time gather information about the designs which can be made from different grades of materials.

'But always have in mind that the pattern is usually only the beginning of the conversation between the engineer and the workman and he is a poor engineer who allows the conversation to stop at the showing of the pattern.

'In fact you might say that this is one way to discover an engineer, to see how much detail he wants to cover with the workman rather than allowing him to use his own judgement on the many hidden sides of the matter, such as the materials which are to be used, the protection that will be given during cartage, or, if the article is of wood, what degree of dryness will be given and what is required.

'But above all remember that you are employing an engineer to *think*, and if your engineer is not a thinker you might as well deal directly with the workmen yourself.

'For example, if you consider the foundations of cathedral walls, it is a matter of considerable difficulty to decide how deep the foundations should be dug, and the inclination of all concerned will be to make them too shallow! The mason will think this way because he will be only too eager to see his beautiful walls appearing and the bishop too will be glad to see early signs of progress! Large holes in the ground are never regarded as progress by the onlookers. An engineer is needed to question sternly the depth which has been decided on – and a good engineer will have a list of cathedral walls which have fallen down, the depth of their foundations and the type of ground.

'If you give me the job of making you a windmill, I will first ask you to pay for a visit to three windmills in Hampshire and Essex, two of which were built by engineer friends of mine. Ten marks in advance would cover the cost.

'Then I will decide on a design, perhaps buying some parts from the man who made the driving wheels for those other mills, and then agree with you the final design and probable cost.'

It was the longest lecture I had had from a man for some years but his suggestion immediately appealed, at least I should be shot of watching those workmen! And before he left I gave him the money and we agreed to meet again in a month's time.

The end of the windmill story is that we built and erected the little windmill in the centre of Louth. It looked quaint and unbalanced and we soon found that it had two main faults. First it was shielded from most winds by the buildings around it so that we were never able to give it a long run. And secondly the pedestal, which had been anchored by covering it with a clay mound quickly shook itself loose so that the whole building juddered alarmingly. Also by this time our engineer had found another job, helping his son on the Palace at Westminster.

Fortunately I received just then a request from the Abbess of Ormsby Priory for a windmill so that she could build up a corn-grinding business and I gladly let her take the mill with the suggestions that she placed it on a clear hill and that the pedestal should be redesigned.

I believe that the windmill is now working very successfully but I have not made too many enquiries in case I am once again brought into contact with a practical machinery matter, which, as I have said, I have no enthusiasm for. The Abbess herself is a completely practical person. At a meeting I was to have with her some six months ago, she made me wait for half an hour while she went away to check, personally, the depth of some new foundations on a small extension which she was having built. When I remonstrated that she should let others do that kind of work she instructed me that with practical work it was wise always to check that what has been reported has actually been done. Particularly with important matters of course and in a building there is probably nothing more important than the foundations. To me this seems unchristian, the Commandments instructing each us not to lie, so that it must be wrong to accuse anyone of lying without first having good cause.

CHAPTER SIX

The Windmill; Edwin Continues his Story

I had come a long way to the east because the roadside gossip was all about strife in the middle lands and the west and that lawless bands were ravaging everything, moving backwards and forwards across the land. And in Northumberland, far to the north, Stephen was fighting the Scots with his northern army. To avoid being robbed or pressed into service (the bands liked to use ex-soldiers, even one-handed ones), I did my best to stay well clear, taking the long way round.

I had little money and, as winter approached, shelter would have to be paid for as well as food. Hedge bottoms give poor comfort in winter in England.

Coming to the top of a rise just off the road, I saw a group of men and two horses standing by the side of a strange hut-like building, and as I drew nearer I saw some heavy timbers lying near.

It was an exposed place. In the valley the air had been still but here there was wind, piercing and gusty, finding thin places and strained seams in my cloak and leggings.

It was the sight of the timbers that halted me, mainly. During my soldiering I had built castles and assault towers as well as forts and had become skilled in the finding and handling of heavy timbers, working in all kinds of weather.

And perhaps the searching wind reminded me of the need to get winter lodgings and to do this I needed a job. I walked towards the little group.

As I got nearer I saw there were six men, one of them talking loudly, in command. The others looked like craftsmen, perhaps carpenters. The talker was broad-shouldered and erect, of middle age, very dark-skinned. One of the men pointed and he turned as I came up. 'We have nothing to give and much to do,' he said loudly. 'Be on your way.' He was a man angry with everyone at that moment. Then he said, no doubt remembering the duty owed to a traveller, 'The nunnery at Ormsby will put you up for the night.'

Even at a distance his voice had seemed familiar, and now a full sight of his great square frame completed the recollection.

'Dennis D'Eath,' I yelled, and he stiffened and became silent as I walked towards him. When I was near his face changed and he shouted, 'Edwin,' and rushed to embrace me. We had soldiered together in Normandy under the Duke and in one fight or another had helped each other to stay alive through the grapplings, wrestlings, fallings and proddings of many skirmishes and battles.

When we had finished patting each other (his carpenters seemed surprised and I remember how they gawped, he had been slanging them hard), he asked what I did in that place. I told him quickly about my journey and my misfortunes and added that I wanted a job.

'You?' he said. 'Out of employ?' He had not noticed my iron hand that I had kept hidden in my cloak. I took it out and raised it in front of his face.

'I had heard something about it,' he said. He had left the duke's army, after serving for twenty years, some little time before I met with my accident.

He looked at me directly, thinking hard. He was a man strong in action, thinking came slowly, but when he had made a plan he always seemed to be able to carry it through.

'Hook or no hook, come and help me here,' he said. So I asked him what was afoot.

'We have here one of the new wind machines for driving millstones. It has been working in Louth for about a year but the abbot is unpleased with the time lost when there is no wind and has decided to gift it to the Nuns of North Ormsby, together with twenty acres of land on this windy hillside. You see there the great 'Box' of the wind machine and we have to build a heavy trestle for it to sit on. Most of the old trestle was worn and rotten and couldn't be moved. It is the design of a new and better trestle that we have to work out.'

'These boys are carpenters, Josh is a millwright. They've no experience with trestles. The digging, burying and joining of all the heavy timbers is in any case not a job they feel able to do. I have nobody else and have never seen it done myself.'

'Dennis,' I said, 'how can a man with one hand help in such a heavy task?'

'Edwin,' he replied, 'I saw you oversee the building of the one hundred foot siege tower at Rimbrant – you remember the one with the pivoted roof – never putting a hand to the work yourself but telling them what to do from that little tumbledown shed at the back of the cookhouse. Even after some ten years I can still recall your plans, scratched on large slabs of slate with figures showing each timber piece. And how you made us measuring sticks and showed us how to use them. Tell us what to do now and I will have it done, perhaps through these lazy rascals or with the help of one or two more from Louth.'

I was interested – and anyway needed the work – and we shook hands on it.

The first thing we did that afternoon was to go back to Louth, to the old site, and look at the parts of the trestle which had been left behind. The construction was simple, a fifteen-inch diameter oak pole was held upright by four leaning supports, all let into the ground so that the earth 'cemented' it all together. It is one of the main features of these wind machines that the house (christened the 'Buck' by the wind machine men) in which the machinery sits and on which the sails are mounted, sits on top of the post and can be moved round to face the wind from whatever direction it blows. As the force from the wind can be high, the post must be very firm if the whole machine is not to be toppled over.

We could see that the Louth trestle had relied for firmness on the large hillock of heavy clay that had been placed round the post. True, there were four leaning supports but these had been displaced by the movement of the post leaving large gaps in three of them between the post and their ends, so that the support they had been giving for some time had been very little.

'It used to judder,' said an old man who came up as we looked at the remains of the trestle, 'Something awful, worst with a north-west wind. Frightened Jake.'

Jake turned out to be the miller, given the job by the abbot after he had looked after Denson's water wheel for many years. He had not liked the change.

It was easy to see that the post had been moving, by several inches, in its clay hole, and that the side supports had been of little use.

I saw that it needed a much stronger framework to support the massive main post, particularly as the new site was windier, and already my mind was on the angles and lengths and the types of joints which would be needed.

By the side of the Ormsby site was a tumbledown sheepfold with a rough hut, its door and shutter missing. It had a place for a fire at one end. I asked Dennis to get his carpenters to make this place fit to live in, so that I would have a place to work in. The carpenters could also use it in bad weather. He grumbled a bit, but had already begun to see that it would be a longer job than he had thought and agreed to do up the hut. He could see too that the little hut in the sheepfold would be useful to the miller as a store.

That night I stayed there, with two candles we got in Louth. It was cold, but before I rolled up in my cloak I had sketched a much stronger trestle on a large flagstone which lay in one corner. The next day I took measurements with a simple rule made from a straight stave divided into thumb-inches and by scaling up from the sketch I could tell Dennis next morning just what timbers we needed for the trestle.

There was straightaway an argument about what to do with the timbers already sent for the buck by the abbot. These were copies of the old trestle timbers. They were all too thin and using them was certain to lead to trouble. With my design we needed more timbers anyway.

As we were arguing – Dennis saw several weeks wasted in waiting for new timbers – a small, very neat lady rode up on a mule and I saw that she was a nun. She was accompanied by a much larger lady, strong rather than neat, also on a mule. Both were known to Dennis and he whispered to me that the neat lady was the Abbess of Ormsby Priory and the other lady was her Reader. The abbess was about forty years old, upright in carriage and very clearly spoken. We quickly found she would not be hurried, and that those who tried got a wave-down from her delicate little hand and something of a frown from her beautiful oval face. We got to know her well during the five months we worked on her wind machine and came to respect her mightily.

She enquired about the dispute, which she had seen as she rode up, noting in particular, as she said evenly, that talking was going on, not work.

We explained about the trestle and the problems with the new timbers to my design. After some sharp questions, particularly about whether it would work (she was not one to spend time chasing moonbeams!) she asked us to meet her the next afternoon at the Louth Abbey, to talk to the abbot, he who had gifted the mill to the nunnery. She passed me an old piece of vellum and told me to clean off the writing and use it to make a drawing of my trestle to show to the abbot. With some trouble I borrowed a small travelling pen and inkhorn from the reader. I noticed that Dennis was listened to carefully by the two ladies and I now found he had been agent at the nunnery for about two years, responding to the reader.

I spent most of the next morning with Dennis in the sheepfold hut (the carpenters had knocked together a rough table), going over my design for the trestle. We tried to use the timbers that had been sent but only the main post was good enough and that was none too long. We needed four supports, ten feet by nine inches square, and two foundation members, sixteen feet by twelve inches by nine inches. The timbers that had been sent were only fit for buried props, not for part of a rigid frame.

At noon we set off for Louth Abbey and arrived in mid-afternoon with the sun low in the western sky. The gatekeeper said that we were expected but that the abbess had not yet arrived and we were invited to the travellers' room where ale and bread was served. I remember it was poor ale and good bread. After a little while, onions and a little smoked fish were given to us from a cupboard in the room.

We had only just finished and it was growing dusk when the gatekeeper came and called us to the abbot's room (lit with many candles!) where we found the abbess who straightaway asked for the drawing. The idea that we might not have done it had not occurred to her; although young she was used to having her own way, and she was just starting to ask us questions when the abbot walked in. He was a tall man, thin in the face, with a busy manner, a man who had much on his mind and many important tasks in hand.

He greeted the abbess, kindly but not looking at her, and she described the problem and told him who we were. Dennis I think he had heard of, mostly good. With me he took a few minutes to ask about my background, and we talked of Normandy and the Duke, whom he had known. Having satisfied himself that he would not be wasting his time on some itinerant rascal (of which there were many in those times), he asked to see the drawing.

He looked at it for several minutes and said nothing. I learned later that he had been one of the best illuminators in England, before accepting promotion, and drawings of all kinds were full of meaning for him.

'It is a miniature, of course,' he said, eventually. 'What is the size of the real thing?' I told him and he ruminated, and then asked a few quick questions that made me glad that the morning had been spent with Dennis going over everything carefully.

After about a quarter of an hour he turned to the abbess and said, 'You were right to raise this matter – nothing would have been gained by attempting the impossible with the old design except temporary relief. Now however we have the problem of finding these heavy timbers quickly so that you can start your milling!'

The abbess raised her beautiful face, ringed with a pure white cowl (the two faces, hers and the abbot's made a striking picture; hers firm and smooth, angelic; his worn and sternly saintly). 'Brother,' she said, 'we have heard that a large fisher boat is being dismantled at Grimsby and that some of its deck and keel members are still fit for use. Is it possible for these to be given to us?' She could have demanded proper new timbers under the agreement, as many would, but she wanted results, not arguments. Always she behaved thus, helping the matter along. Now he looked at her, then at Dennis. 'Would they be suitable?' he asked, and Dennis looked at me, and we finished up agreeing to go to Grimsby the next day to look at the timbers.

Next day they lent us mules and we set off at first light, having spent the night in the travellers' rooms at the abbey. By late afternoon we had examined the timbers, laid out on the shore as they were, and had agreed what we wanted. There was a problem with curvature in some of the timbers but I could see this as an advantage, with proper joints. The wood was oak, by far the best for the purpose.

By using the names of the abbot and abbess freely we managed to get the timbers promised for the next day, the carter being well used to taking timbers from the wreckers' yards at Grimsby to sites all over the county, mainly for use in house building. He grumbled that he had passed our site last week on the way back from Lincoln and that his horses were not yet rested.

We got back to the abbey before midnight, the mules having been bad tempered as only mules can be when worked too hard.

Next day we went by foot to Elkington and by noon were instructing the carpenters in the work which had to be done to receive the timbers.

First I wanted two deep trenches dug to receive the thick cross timbers which had been the ship's keel. And at the bottom of each trench I asked for a layer of stones to be laid so that the timbers would drain and not rot with the wet. There was no shortage of stones on the hillside. Then we would put up a three-legs to haul the heavy post into position and hold it there until we could get the side supports into position. The three-legs had to come from the nunnery, where Dennis had been carrying out work on the foundations of a new chapel, and he had scaffolding poles and a lifting pulley ready to bring.

It was the end of November before the trestle was finished and the weather had turned bad. Driving rain and cold made work impossible for long periods so we finished it off by warming ourselves in the sheepfold and then dashing out for short spells of work. For a week after that we could only huddle round the fire in the hut (we used heather roots mainly and they burned badly) but sometimes struggled into Louth to an ale-house. And then, about the middle of December, the weather eased and became calm and dry and not too cold. We mounted the buck on the post and finished off all the carpentry work during the first five days of fine weather.

During the bad weather we had argued endlessly about how to put the buck on the top of the post. I was for taking it apart, and then, after mounting the crown trees which pivoted on top of the post, rebuilding it again in position. Others thought we could lift the whole buck and sit it down again on the post.

It depended on whether our lifting gear could handle the load. (When they took it down at Louth they had the heavy tripod from the abbey's masonry department.) In the end we compromised, stripping the buck down to its frame and removing all the machinery. We did this on the first two days of good weather and on the third day lifted it with no difficulty to sit on the post. Matthew the carpenter left then to go to another job, leaving Clacky his apprentice to help with the final fitting out.

The work I had agreed to do myself was now finished but it was the middle of winter and the sheepfold hut was fairly habitable so I offered to stay on and supervise the rest of the work until the mill was running. All I asked for as a wage was fuel for the fire and food and ale. I explained to Dennis that this would release him for other work in Ormsby and the reader agreed readily to the suggestion.

They had given me two marks for designing the trestle so that for a time at least I had no need to worry about the future.

Perhaps the most important man concerned with the mill was Josh the millwright. He had had experience with five of these wind machines during the last four or five years and was rightly seen as the local expert. His workshop was part of the blacksmith's shop at Louth and he had a little donkey to carry his tools.

After he had seen us start work on the trestle, Josh came to Dennis and said that as there would be nothing for him to do for a time he would go to another job at Hogsthorpe and come back when we were ready.

Before he went, Dennis made sure that any changes he wanted to the buck had been described to Matthew the carpenter – the main one, as it turned out, being the raising of the main bearing of the wind-shaft so that the shaft would be slightly tilted.

About this tilting, Josh said, 'If you don't tilt it up, any wear will make it tilt down so that it will be pulled away from the lantern pinion.'

And on balancing, Josh said, 'Don't bother to balance the buck. When I get the machinery in that will be the time to try to get a balance.'

Although we had not sent for him, Josh returned just as Matthew was going, after we had put the buck on top of the post. He straightaway got to work, fitting the main bearings to the shaft while both were on the ground. The bearings were of iron – an expensive part – and these had to be a good running fit round the smooth ash shaft. The large brake wheel was already in position on the shaft, being keyed in place by four ash wedges.

The three of us managed to raise the wind-shaft into position, using a rope passed through an eye in the roof beam, and it sat down readily into its bearings and could easily be turned by hand.

'Grease is the secret,' said Josh, 'the miller's friend and enemy! Without plenty of grease on the bearings and gears much of the force of the wind will go into the machinery instead of into the corn. But many a miller has been caught up in the running machinery and killed when leaning over to grease the parts.'

'What grease?' I asked and Josh grinned. 'I make it up myself,' he said, 'and sell it to the millers. It's my own mix and I'm not going to tell you how it's made.' Then, relenting a little, 'Mutton fat, lard and some black lead, but in what parts is my secret.' Later on my journey, I found that Josh's grease was known about as far away as York.

The old sailcloth was thin and worn and the abbess had told me to get some new cloth from the sister nunnery at Grimsby where they wove sailcloth. I helped Josh lace the

cloth onto the sail-frames before hoisting the frames into place on the wind-shaft. We had furled them in case of a sudden squall although there was no wind at the time.

The lantern pinion was in good condition and was soon fitted. The stones took longer, great care being necessary if they were not to swing against parts of the buck and become chipped. The passage for them through the buck door and up to the milling floor was twisting and awkward.

The tail-pole had been fitted by the carpenters before they left and we spent two days balancing the machine so that it could be easily turned by one man leaning on the tail-pole. In the end we had a row of large stones in the buck, on the side away from the sails, to balance the weight of the sails and gears. When the mill was running the miller might be able to replace the stones with bags of flour, or so Josh said.

Josh instructed me, 'You have to be more skilled than a ship's captain to run a mill. A mill can't bend to the wind like a ship and, if a tail wind hits it, the whole thing might be lifted off the post as well as the sails broken. A miller has to watch for changes of wind as much as any ship's captain and squalls can be much more dangerous for him. He tries to keep the sails facing the wind and to furl the sails if the wind gets too strong but he is often caught out when the weather is blustery. Tends to make them bitter. Many are hurt or killed when they try to disengage gears in a sudden storm.'

'Lightning is another thing,' said Josh. 'Windmills are usually the highest things in the area – they have to be to catch the wind – and lightning always goes for the highest object. One miller in Essex was killed this way and others have been stunned.'

It was near to the end of January before Josh had everything to his liking. We had a week of very cold frosty weather with absolutely no wind, but at that time of the year when the wind came it was likely to be strong and stormy. The nunnery had arranged for Jake, the miller from Louth, to run their mill for a while, until another miller could be found. He was not easy about it, having taken against it because of the judder, but the new trestle impressed him and he agreed to try it.

Jake took about a week to go over all the arrangements we had made and to grease and clean all the bearings. He lifted the top stone and spent a few hours fettling the grooves that were not to his liking. On the last day of January he agreed that we could have a trial the next day and Dennis promised to have some corn brought along from the nunnery.

With the corn, the abbess, the reader, and two nuns also arrived next morning, eager to see their mill in action. The wind was fairly steady from the north-west and we swung the mill round and set the sails half-reefed.

Jake slowly let off the brake and the mill began to turn for the first time on its new site.

Jake and Josh were inside the buck and I was outside with the abbess, watching the sails. I had never seen a windmill work before, but it seemed too noisy and I was not surprised when the sails stopped turning after a short time and Josh appeared at the door of the buck.

'Pinions jumping under load,' he said. 'We'll have to move the bearing.'

I stayed out. There was little space inside the buck and Jake and Josh were already banging away in there. After five minutes they tried again.

'Watch out,' they cried and the sails began to turn again. This time it was quieter and the rumblings were regular, almost musical, like a trumpet on its lowest note. The abbess smiled, believing that now everything would be well.

The abbess wanted the mill to have a name, a name suitable for a mill owned by a nunnery, but also striking, because it was the first mill in these parts.

The abbess and the reader talked together quietly about whether to ask the abbot or hold a meeting about it in the nunnery, but the abbess suddenly said, 'No, I will have my way on this; it shall be called "Little Giant".'

And so it became known far and wide.

Little Giant ran well. In three months, (before I set off on my travels again), we produced 320 hundredweight of coarse flour and 400 hundredweight of cattle meal for the nunnery. Fine meal for making the best bread was not possible with the stones we had and the abbess had yet to decide whether to send for French burr stones.

The way in which the nuns arranged a steady flow of corn, without large amounts being held up anywhere was interesting and Jake was full of praise for their skill. About other matters he was more critical, feeling that he was being asked to behave like a machine himself to produce what was wanted.

I worked with him, mostly moving sacks, but sometimes helping with the stone dressing (which was tricky and lost us a lot of time), all for my keep – good food, generously provided by the nuns – and the promise of a 'present' when I left.

When the first hedgerow flowers started to show at the end of March I decided to move on.

CHAPTER SEVEN

Assistance from a Bishop and an Abbess

From Elkington I made my way north and ferried across the Humber on the fourth day. People were on the move, at this, the end of winter, with the roads drying up and the days longer. Most were on foot but the tradesmen had their donkeys and one or two four-wheeled carts were carrying stone and building materials, all going north. From time to time horsemen in small groups passed quickly by and I was often forced off the road.

That morning – it was a glorious spring morning – I found myself walking by the side of a large cart drawn by four bullocks. The driver was at the head of the offside leader and although the cart seemed empty they appeared to be hard-pressed. After a while he noticed me and shouted, 'Can'st lead?' and I shrugged off my pack and threw it onto the front of the cart and then went round to the near side and took hold of the other leading bullock.

We went fairly well for about four or five miles, when, the day being warm now, the driver decided to stop and rest his team. We pulled off into the shelter of a willow thicket, unhitched the bullocks and hobbled them so that they could look for some soft shoots, and we sat down on the edge of the cart. While we ate our bait he told me his story.

His name was Jon, and he said that people often called him Jon of the Stanes. He was chief carter for a quarry in the Wolds owned by the Bishop of Beverley. He had never had any other work, having been born by the quarry and then working in it from being a boy. When he was twelve, he had made his first long journey, with his father, to London. They carried two large lintel stones for a new abbey in Westminster. On the way back his father was taken ill and died of the plague in a rest-shed at the back of an ale-house in Bury. Jon brought the four bullocks and cart back himself and for the rest of his life could not remember much about the journey.

Once we had exchanged a few words he moved to the offside lead bullock to examine it carefully.

It was called Nant and was his best bullock, having been in work for some ten years.

As he ran his hands over the great animal, he whistled a slow tune, to soothe it, and I remembered then the farrier at Douai whistling the same tune when he tended the Prince's black warhorse before the fight at Pont Dracon.

The bullock had been sluggish on the march, but was now restless, shifting from foot to foot and shaking its head.

Jon shook his own head: 'He is troubled with a big lump in his belly and perhaps it now touches something vital,' he said sadly.

As he spoke the bullock threw back its head sharply, then its legs folded and it rolled over. Like all dead creatures, it suddenly looked smaller.

Jon wasted no time in grieving over his old friend. 'When this happened once before, at a place near Lincoln, I sold the dead beast to a local butcher. He said he wanted it for his lord's deerhounds but it probably finished up on his meat counter. While I stay here will you go to that village we came through and offer the beast at the butcher's shop which I saw at the other end of the village?'

I walked back to the shop which was set back from the main street with a holding paddock in front. The butcher, a small old man, and his young assistant were cutting up a sheep on the board at the side of the shop. I stated my business and asked for an offer.

To my surprise he looked embarrassed and glanced over his shoulder at a tall man standing in the shade of the shop who immediately came to me and asked, 'Are you offering a dead animal for sale to this butcher?' When I said that I was he gave a shrill whistle and two men came from the back of the shop and took hold of my arms.

'I am the deputy sheriff for the parish,' he said, 'and I am placing you under arrest for offering carcass meat to anyone except the estate steward, contrary to the law.' The butcher looked at me and nodded. I could see that the law was not one he approved of, but there was nothing he could do.

The dungeon where I was lodged was of a kind common in small castles of the countryside. A hole about twenty feet across, dug about six feet deep with a wall of tightly packed posts arranged all round the edge to a height of about twelve feet. A roughly thatched roof completed the building except for the entrance, which was small, and, of course, some six feet above the level of the floor. The door was a solid block of timber sliding up and down in deep grooves in two posts. The jailers lighted a large torch before they opened the door, for the most part so they could see into the large black hole, in which there were no windows, but the torch was also a weapon in case prisoners rushed the door, a difficult feat in any case because of the six foot drop. For most prisoners the fall down the six foot drop was their first taste of prison life, the scrapes and shock being only small preparation for the real cruelties yet to come as the prisoners rotted in the damp pit. It was common to hear a dungeon of this kind described as the local 'Jump'.

I stood still as the dungeon door was dropped and tried to peer through the blackness. Before I had been pushed I had had time to see a number of bundles round the wall and now wondered how to contact any life that might exist.

'Over here, lad,' said a voice. 'I need some new company.' The voice was strong but not unfriendly, and I moved cautiously in that direction. A hand guided me to a stone seat that ran round the edge – the only 'furniture' in the dungeon. 'Yon other two are speechless, they are to hang in the morning, and the bundle the other side of you spends most of his time asleep.'

He was a cottager, called Matthew and was in the dungeon because of an argument with the steward of his lord's estate.

Part of his rent was twenty planks, 'of good seasoned wood without shakes' and an argument over one of the planks, which the steward had refused to accept, finished up with the steward being felled with the same plank. 'I am a strong man, seldom angry,' he said, 'but that new steward would try the patience of a saint.' He thought he would escape with a stiff fine when he came up before the manorial court.

He had been in the dungeon for two months, the manorial court having been delayed because of a royal visit. His chief worry was not the fine but the gradual weakening of his frame because of the lack of exercise and the problem he would have in returning to his heavy work about the farm.

That evening we were handed a basin of thick gruel with five wooden spoons and a jug of water, these being lowered down on a tray at the end of a rope. There was plenty because Matthew and I were the only ones interested. The criminals crawled over and took a swig of water though, without a word.

After about an hour the jailer opened the door, shouted for the things to be put back on the tray and hauled it up. The door was closed for the night and I could start to carry out my plan of escape.

During my soldiering, I had built a dozen or more dungeons of this kind. It was the simplest type, after a plain paddock, and popular when heavy wood was easily obtainable. The weakest place was at the join between the upright wall posts and the roof and I had no doubt that I would find a place to get through if I could get up there.

The sheriff's men had laughed at my hook and then ignored it and, after a quick word with Matthew, I started to score deep grooves to make shallow footholds in two neighbouring posts. It was heavy work and for the last six feet I had to cling onto a groove with my fingers, my toes in a lower groove, while I made the next groove.

It was nearly dawn when I finally hauled myself onto the tops of the post-wall and after that it only took a few minutes to squeeze under the roof and drop down the outside of the wall. No one stirred. I crept silently to the surrounding fence, climbed it and stole off into the half-light.

It took me an hour to reach the place where I had left Jon with his cart and dead bullock. The bullock was still lying there but Jon and the cart were gone. I guessed that he had sensed trouble – there was plenty about in those days – and had set off again as fast as he could. I followed as quickly as I might along the same road.

It was important for me to catch up with him as soon as possible because all my kit including my discharge chits were on the cart where I had left them when I went to see the butcher. Without a chit of any kind I would be in trouble if any sheriff's man should stop me. So in spite of a night in which I had been in a constant sweat with hard work, I went at what was a running stumble northward after Jon, taking my first bearing from the North Star which was just visible in the lightening sky. I had not gone more than a mile before I saw the cart before me and managed to climb aboard to fall into the sleep of utter exhaustion – such a sleep as soldiers sleep after a long battle.

The jogging and rumbling of the cart finally woke me just before noon and I hailed Jon who was plodding along beside the remaining lead bullock. 'I saw you get on,' he said, 'but could see that you wanted to sleep. Besides, there was no time to be wasted in getting out of that parish – it is well known for its strange laws and hostility to travellers. Now we are safe and I will pull up at a place I know in about half a mile.'

My kit was still lying on the front of the cart and I lost no time in checking my papers and other things. Everything was in order and I was thankful that the driver I had fallen in with, Jon, had proved to be an honest man.

We stopped by a little field with a tidy hovel and a small brook. An ancient cottager welcomed us and we paid a groat for the animals to graze and for a loaf of leavened bread and a piece of cottage cheese. The sun was warm for the first time that year and we lay back on the cart and ate our meal and talked at intervals. I remember that at one point he asked what would happen to Matthew if it was thought he had helped me to escape – as indeed he had – and I told him that Matthew had asked me to give him a slight head wound so that he could explain that I had attacked him. Jon asked what I was going to do now and I told him I was going to get Matthew out of the dungeon.

Just before I had left the windmill project, the prioress had asked me to visit her at the nunnery and when I arrived I was escorted to her office, where I was surprised to see the abbot sitting down beside her.

'Edwin,' the prioress said, 'we are sorry to see you go but understand that you have a duty to proceed to your home country. The abbot and I believe that much of the success of the windmill has been due to your work and management and we have prepared a document which might help you on your travels. It is in Latin, but it is addressed to those in charge of monasteries and nunneries and asks them to help you if they can on your travels.'

This was a magnificent present. It meant that I would get very favourable treatment at all the religious guest-houses until I arrived at my home.

The time had now come to test the real worth of this document.

The cottager informed me that there was a nunnery some five miles to the west, which I would reach if I followed the path alongside the little brook. I said goodbye to Jon and set off for the nunnery.

It was a big place constructed mostly of timber (well constructed too, as my builder's eye could see!), but it had a little chapel made of chiselled stone. After a few preliminaries I was conducted to the abbess, an old, very tall lady, richly dressed with silver at her throat and waist, who read the document prepared by the prioress, slowly and with care.

'We are glad to welcome you, my son,' she said. 'What is it you want from us?'

I described my unpleasant experience in the dungeon in the next parish and she became stern and after a moment's thought said, 'I do not see how I can help an escaped criminal but I will consult with the bishop who is here today on his annual tour of inspection. Perhaps this will take his mind off some of the chatterings of our young initiates about the way I run this nunnery.'

It was only afterwards, in conversation with the bailiff for the parish that I learnt how fortunate I had been in the timing of my meeting with the abbess. The bishop's practice was to interview each nun separately and encourage them to talk

78

freely about all their problems – real or otherwise. Usually he finished up with a thousand small matters which had to be discussed in full with the abbess, a process which both found extremely tedious. The matter I was raising was not only important in itself but gave the bishop some much needed material to attack the stewardship of Dennis de Bentley in the next parish. It was an opportunity he had been seeking for some time, as he was repeatedly reminded of Bentley's misgovernment by complaints of travellers who had been forced to flee the parish or who were brought up as vagrants in the church court.

After an hour or so I was led in front of the bishop, who had in his possession the letter from the prioress and my discharge from the duke.

I told my tale again and pointedly included Matthew and the reason he had been locked up for so long.

He decided, there and then, to travel to see de Bentley the next day and, a little reluctantly, I agreed to go with him. I slept in the nunnery guest house and was on the road with the bishop's train early next morning.

At the Manor House we were met at the gate in the palisade by the steward, Baldwin, who, after the usual obeisances, offered to take the bishop to De Bentley. The bishop was very stiff and said that he wished his travelling companions to go with him, and that he wished De Bentley to have his officers with him, for he was determined to chastise the heartless steward before an audience.

We trooped into the hall of the castle and, as no one had thought to warn De Bentley, we came on him, sitting in a large chair before the log fire, with a jug of wine at his elbow.

When he heard the noise of our entrance he looked over his shoulder and then, seeing the bishop in his scarlet cloak, attempted to stand. The first time was not successful, and he sank back, but the next time he got up although he had to cling to the back of the chair for support.

'I pray forgiveness, your excellency,' he spluttered, his speech blurred and from one side of his mouth. He sat down abruptly. The bishop stood before him without saying a word.

'My lord has been unwell,' said Baldwin. 'He is now not able to leave the room and everything has to be done for him.'

'I was not told of this,' said the bishop. 'Who rules here while he is sick?'

'I myself try to do so,' said Baldwin, 'but it is not easy, in these changing times.'

I have since thought of Baldwin as a good man in a very difficult position rather than wicked.

'My lord has insisted that his illness should not be broadcast, but for the last two months it has been very difficult because, as you see, he now cannot find it in himself to be normal. Apart from the effects of his stroke, he is nearly always drunk.'

He thought for a moment. 'He has been a good master to all of us, and we know not where to turn. The earl, his master, is at Winchester and never comes so far north. Under his direction. we have been well fed and peaceful for many years. The dungeon has been empty and the manorial court a formality. I have striven to maintain his rule while he has been ill but in his absence and lacking his insight and strong bearing I have had to fall back on a strict enforcement of our old local laws, some of which we have not used for many years.

'The collection of rents has been very difficult for me. My master knew how to handle the matter so that each was satisfied, taking into account the changing times, but I have no authority except my recollection of the old agreements which of course were always verbal.'

'I have a man in the dungeon now who has been a faithful cottager on my lord's estate for many years, and his father before him. [He was talking about Matthew.] He was due to pay some of his rent in planks although, with the dearth of trees in the area, planks are now hard to come by. He did his best but was unable to satisfy my deputy even after submitting three separate lots of planks. My master would have been able pass the matter off and take something available, and perhaps more valuable, from Matthew, but I had to stick to the law and insist that Matthew pay the exact rent. In the end he was so exasperated that he struck my deputy and I had to put him in the jump – I mean the dungeon.'

'And what about jailing this man?' said the bishop, pointing to me. 'How can a man be jailed for offering a carcass for sale?'

'That is simple,' replied Baldwin. 'When we had a bad flux which killed off people some ten years ago my master put it down to people eating beefs which had died of the foot and mouth disease, and he made a law that all animals which had died a natural death should be first offered to him, so that he could have them inspected for obnoxious diseases.'

'It seems a good law,' said the bishop dryly, 'but not one which a stranger would be likely to know about.'

'Please take your lord to his bed,' continued the bishop, 'and provide me with writing materials. With your permission, I will use your lord's great table as my desk.'

He dictated two letters to the scribe who was in his train. The first was to the earl in Winchester describing the state of affairs in the parish. The second was to the steward, Baldwin, to say that he proposed that day to hold a church court to try those impeached by Baldwin, including, of course, those in the dungeon and myself.

I was the first case and the bishop merely warned me that as a newly returned soldier it would well behove me to make sure of my legal position in any business venture before attempting it. Many laws had changed in the last thirty years and many local laws had been made by local rulers. With this I was dismissed.

As I was crossing the courtyard I saw Matthew being led in. I waved to him and he returned my salute. I asked permission to await the outcome of Matthew's trial.

He was out within ten minutes and we walked together through the gate. When I asked for news of his trial he said that Baldwin himself had submitted that Matthew's term in the dungeon was adequate punishment. The bishop had immediately agreed and Matthew was dismissed.

We walked slowly down the road in the bright spring sunshine. The hedgerows were coming into leaf with flowers at the roadside – primroses, violets, ragged robin. Matthew walked very slowly. He was weak and needed time to get used to the light, and even the mildest exercise. I offered to see him home.

After two miles, we turned off the main road and walked going down a narrow lane to a thatched cottage that had tidy sheds on three sides. No one was in and Matthew sat down heavily on a chair inside the door and asked me to try to find his wife or son. From the back of the house I saw two figures hoeing at the other end of a small field and at my shout one of them, who turned out to be the sixteen years old son, came running towards me. Quickly all was explained, and he hailed his mother, then dashed to the front of the house to see his father. I waited for the mother, told her the news briefly, and escorted her round the house. I waited in the yard for the family to get over its first raptures.

After ten minutes, I began to think that I should move on and was actually starting to walk away towards the road, when Matthew hobbled out of the house and yelled hoarsely, 'Don't go, Edwin, I have something to ask.'

What he suggested was that I should stay with them for the summer. I would be treated as an honoured guest and additionally any work I did on his little farm would be paid for at the highest rates.

After a little thought, I accepted. Amongst other things, I was anxious to make sure that Baldwin would manage things properly until help arrived from the earl.

CHAPTER EIGHT

Matthew a Tenant Farmer;
Edwin is Beaten Up

Matthew had for his own use about eight acres fit for cropping, and about two acres of rough rocky land only good for pigs. He was obliged to work for his lord for two days a week, and because of his skill as a builder, this was mainly repair work on the estate buildings. In particular he was a good carpenter and spent much of his time in such work. (It was because of his skill in carpentry that the argument with the steward about the plank was particularly bitter.) His weakness after his imprisonment meant that he would, for a time, be very limited as to the work he could do.

He kept two cows and a pig that usually had a litter and all but two of the young pigs were passed to the estate when they were three-parts grown. The family ate meat once a week, their normal meals being hot vegetable stew from the stewpot that was always on the fire. Sometimes they had bread or an egg. While he was in the dungeon, Matthew's wife had given two of the sow's last litter to the jailer so that Matthew could have better food, and the two remaining piglets were due to be sent to the estate that very day as rent due.

I was given a straw bed in the shed next to the house and saw that this would suit me very well for the summer. I pleaded tiredness – I had had two nights without sleep – and in any case Matthew wanted some time with his wife. I slept soundly for three or four hours. When I awoke I could hear voices in the house and being very hungry went to see what food and drink could be got.

Matthew, his wife and son were there. Matthew welcomed me warmly. As the light was fading they had lit two or three rushlights and in this light, and the light of the fire, I sat down at a little three-legged table to a bowl of good stew, a large piece of bread and a tankard of ale. I ate quickly and soon was ready to talk, which I knew they were waiting for.

While I ate, I had a good look at Matthew's wife. Her name was Mary and she was a large strong-looking woman with a round face which was sturdy in the eyes and mouth. Her nose was small and upturned. Her brown hair was in two pigtails, one at each side of her head. She had been working in the field all day, and after the excitement of seeing Matthew return was now looking sleepy.

The son, as might be expected from these two parents, was strongly built and although only sixteen was equal in build and height to many men. He too was exhausted, having had to work twice as hard as usual during Matthew's absence, and the late spring work had been particularly heavy because of the wet weather.

It was no time of day for a serious discussion about anything and I suggested that we should all go to bed and have a talk in the morning.

Next day, when we were breaking our fast on bread and weak ale, Matthew broke the silence. 'Edwin,' he said, 'we owe you a great deal for getting me out of that dungeon. It is difficult for us to repay you but we see you as a man who has no urgent plans and who might like to spend the summer with us. We shall be glad to feed you and provide you with shelter. Should you feel like helping on the farm we'll try to pay you, but please take notice that payment is likely to be in kind, we seldom see coin here. When you leave you can hardly take a quarter of a sheep with you!'

Mary joined in: 'It might be better, if you are willing, for you to undertake the estate work for which Matthew is bound. No one works as hard at estate work as on their own land!'

I could see that she would like to have Matthew very near her for some time.

They were generous in their offers, as generous as they were able to be, with the farm work behind and the estate work owing.

I would have none of it. 'Matthew,' I said, 'the estate owes us both something for wrongful arrest and I will first try to strike a bargain with Baldwin for my services so that I can then contribute to my keep in your cottage. I would very much like to stay with you for the summer, the litter in the hut at the side will suit me very well for a sleeping place, and Mary's cooking is something I am certain to enjoy. But I insist on paying my way so I will go to Baldwin immediately to see what I can arrange.'

They tried to dissuade me. They had no faith in Baldwin or his justice and feared that the business of Matthew and the plank might be reopened. We talked around, for some time and it was left that I should try my luck with Baldwin.

They went with me to the castle gate and after I had stated my business I heard a coarse voice ask loudly inside, 'Does he want to go back into the jump?'

After about half an hour I was conducted to Baldwin.

He was one of those thin tall men who by constant striving often obtain promotion even when they do not have the qualities normally found in leaders. He was, as he had shown during his brief spell of authority, of a clerkly disposition, happy with rules, not with making them.

He sat in an armchair in the great hall and kept me standing in front of him.

'You are that man who was arrested by my sheriff and pardoned by the bishop, yesterday?' he asked.

'That I was pardoned should be enough,' I answered.

'Perhaps.' His clerkly mind was searching his rule book to find a way to embarrass me or worse.

'I have here a letter from the brother of your earl, in whose army I served as a soldier and under-officer for twenty-five years. It asks for safe passage for me from all who value his favour.'

Baldwin's attitude changed. This was more powerful than his rule book, or at least gave him a stronger rule to consider.

He read the letter and then handed it back, silently. 'What do you wish from me?' he said.

I gave him my view that the arrests of Matthew and myself were wrongful and due to faulty moves on his part; that I was much disposed to seek redress from a higher authority but that I would bargain with him for a different solution. I then explained that I wished to live with Matthew and his wife for the summer but that I required a job so that I could pay for their hospitality; that I was reasonably good at building work and carpentry and that I could carry out the work normally done by Matthew; that Matthew was not fit for work because of his long imprisonment. As compensation for our wrongful imprisonment I would expect to be paid for my work, even though Matthew was obliged to do the work free as part of his rent. In other words, I was asking for four months' paid work for myself, and the release of Matthew from this part of his rent.

He looked at me for a long time. His lean face had gone very white.

'For one who, in my view, should still be in my dungeon, you are over-forceful,' he said, and paused for thought. 'However I have decided that my master would be in sympathy with your views, and after the lecture and letter I had from the bishop yesterday I am now inclined to guess what my master would do in the circumstances and not just consult my rule book.'

'You will report to the estate carpenter on Monday and Tuesday each week and you may tell Matthew that he is excused his estate work for four months.'

'And the pay?'

'Five pence per day. I shall get reports from my carpenter each week and reductions will be made for any shoddy work.'

My news was received with much satisfaction by Matthew and his wife. 'We shall be able to work together on hoeing and light work until you get your strength back,' she said. She brought out a small barrel of strong ale and we all drank a tankard-ful before eating a large basin of her special mutton stew for dinner.

It was Saturday when I saw Baldwin, and I spent the evening making my sleeping hut shipshape and going through my things. My cloak and leggings were very muddy after falling into the dungeon and my shoes needed stitching. My hair was long and dirty, I had lost my hat altogether, and my undershirt clung to my body.

Matthew pointed out a bathing place in the river, and I went down a grassy path and stripped off on the bank before walking into the river. It was quite cool but I stayed in for some time, thinking about things. I had never learned to swim but I walked up and down in the clear water, the feel of mud between my toes feeling very good. I sat on the bank for a while before washing my undershirt in the river. Carrying my clothes and with only my cloak round me, I went back to my hut and sat on my straw bed before starting to brush off my other clothes. Finally I got out my needle and thread and sewed up my shoes. Having dressed I went round to the cottage door and asked Matthew and Mary to tell me how to get to the ale-house.

It was kept by an old soldier called Denney who told me in the first minute that he had soldiered everywhere in the world but when I mentioned some of the places in France and Italy where I had seen fighting he became quiet. There was one other man in the ale-house, sitting by himself at a trestle table. I could not see him clearly, in the dim light, but sat down at the table and said, 'Good day, friend.'

To my astonishment he jumped to his feet and shouted, 'Edwin!'

I was slow to know him. He was younger than me and had a new scar from his right temple to his chin. I must have looked puzzled. 'Bailey,' he said. 'Don't you remember, your assistant at Charlesroi?'

It all came back – how I had selected him as an assistant from half a dozen men suggested by the prince because of his liveliness and the directness of his gaze. And how we had together designed and had assembled the siege machines during three months of siege. The tall towers had been the worst, fifty feet high and with eight wheels; and tracks too which could be quickly laid for them to roll on. He had finished the design for these when I went down with fever and, when they were made and used, they worked well.

I embraced him warmly. We had worked together for long hours over three months, under heavy pressure from the prince. We knew each other's strengths and weaknesses as well as any man can know such things. We drifted apart after the city was taken and I had not seen him since.

'I am retired,' he explained, 'because of this wound to my head, which makes me dizzy sometimes. It was shortly after you yourself left, in the act of quelling a riot in Biene. A butcher's last act before he died from a spear thrust was to hurl his cleaver at me. For a time they thought I was dead.'

We talked till the torches burned down. He had a bed in the ale-house and had been there five nights. We arranged to meet again the next week.

Next day was Sunday and in the morning I set off to mass with Matthew and Mary. John pleaded fatigue and stayed at home.

It was when we were on the main road, between two high hedges, that the attack took place.

We were going slowly, Mary and I both helping Matthew who was still weak, and I was quite unprepared.

They came from our right side, four of them, wielding clubs. An early blow caught me on the head and I can only dimly recall the rest – very many, blows and kicks to all parts of my body.

I came round slowly and in great pain but forced myself to sit up and look around. Matthew was sat down in the road, holding his head. Mary was standing, but clutching her left arm and crying. There was no sign of our attackers.

With great difficulty, all supporting each other in any way we could, we managed to get back to the cottage and sent John for the sheriff. Matthew and I lay on the floor, too weak and sore to move any further. Mary sat weeping in a chair. By good fortune John met two women from a nearby farm who were on their way to church and they came in and set about tending our hurts. Mary's arm, which was broken, was set with a splint and bandaged with a paste of comfrey, and our bruises and cuts were cleaned and sponged. We crawled to our beds. When the sheriff came about an hour later we were too tired to say much and in any case had very little to tell him.

In the evening, following a day that we had all spent on our beds, there was a shout outside and my friend from Charlesroi, Bailey, appeared. 'Edwin,' he shouted, 'are you all right?' I barked something (my lips were bruised) and he came in and looked down at me. 'Do you want to tell me what happened?' he asked.

For the first time since the attack I felt able to pull myself together and a number of things started to become clear which I started to list.

Robbery had not been the aim, nothing had been taken, and we had been desperately punished but deliberately not killed.

I started to find that I had a remembrance of words spoken during the attack. (Few men can fight without uttering.) ' "Get the soldier first," ' or something like that, just as the first blow fell. ' "Don't kill them." "Leave the woman." ' And then when I had been beaten and kicked into near-unconsciousness, ' "Enough, separate, meet again at Derringby tomorrow." '

One spoke with a Scotch accent, another with a accent that was perhaps Dutch.

Although my strength was returning, I found it tiring to talk. 'Find out where Derringby is and come back in the morning,' I asked him. 'Leave me now.'

The women came back to see us in the evening and brought milk and cakes. I spent a restless night, being unable to lie at ease, and groans from the cottage reached me from time to time to tell me that Matthew was in a similar state.

I was sitting on my straw bed when Bailey came soon after sun-up. 'Derringby is a run-down ale-house about five miles away, the other side of the great wood,' he told me. 'It is said that the owner is a young brother of Baldwin's brought up by him after their father died.'

And it came clearly to my mind, at that moment, that we had not been attacked by a gang of masterless men, but by trained men, men practised in skirmishing and ambuscade, who could work together as a team. Baldwin, who had been long in his post, would have friends in neighbouring sokes who would be willing to provide sheriff's men to punish one who had set his face against his authority; perhaps led by one of his own men.

The ale-house keeper had a little donkey that I had seen him feeding on my visit and I asked Bailey to go and borrow it. When he returned (he had asked a hire charge of one penny for the day) I asked to be lifted onto its back and in great pain got Bailey to lead me to the nunnery. It was no part of my plan but I fell off the donkey unconscious at the nunnery gate and had to be carried in by two porters.

When I became aware again of my surroundings I saw that I was in one of their little whitewashed cells lying on something soft, with a pillow, and covered by a thick blanket. After a little time an elderly nun came in. She saw that I was awake and told me not to talk, but that she would bring me a drink that would send me to sleep for the night. She said that my friend had returned home with the donkey.

Next morning I was gently wakened by the same nun, who got me up and helped me to a room where I could clean myself. Afterwards she took me back to the cell and after another drink – this time a long drink of cool milk – asked me to tell her what had happened. When I had done so, I asked if I could see the prioress on a matter of importance and after a short time she came into my cell. She told me not to get up and we talked while I squirmed on the pallet (even talking was painful, with my bruised lips and the pain in my chest), and she stood alongside.

She agreed to write a letter straight away to the bishop setting out both what had happened to me and my suspicions about the identity of the attackers. She told me to rest until we had a reply, which she hoped to have by noon the following day.

Another sleeping draught in the evening took me through the night and I awoke the next morning in less pain and more determined than ever to see justice done.

Just as the bell rang for matins (I can remember it was badly cracked!), an elderly nun with a face as rosy as a Normandy apple brought me a small loaf, crusty and delicious, and a jug of sweet ale. She said that the prioress would visit me at three Holy Mary candles but that the candles were bad, having been made from dirty wax, and that I must be ready for a visit any time during the afternoon.

When she came, I was able to rise but felt glad when she told me to sit down.

Her messenger had brought her a reply to the letter to the bishop from his chancellor to say that the bishop was still on tour but that he himself would arrive at De Bentley's castle in two days' time, on Friday, to hold an enquiry. He asked that Matthew, Mary and I should all be there and said that he himself would arrange for Baldwin and his brother from Derringby to attend.

I stayed in the nunnery until early morning on Friday, most of the time resting in the little white cell and being attended to by the little rosy-cheeked nun. When Bailey came to see me on Thursday morning I asked him to go and tell Matthew and Mary about the chancellor's enquiry the next day and to make sure that they would be there. I said I would meet them at the castle gate an hour before noon.

The court was held in the hall of De Bentley's castle and started soon after midday. The chancellor was a stern-faced broadly built man who never smiled, younger than I had expected. The proceedings were formal, everything under oath and written down by his own scribe.

Matthew, Mary and I were examined in turn and we each had to tell everything we remembered about the attack. I was closely examined about what the attackers had uttered during the assault, and as I was being questioned, it suddenly came into my mind that as they rushed towards us one of them had shouted, 'The one with the hook.' At this the chancellor had the scribe note that he found it important that the attackers knew that I had a hook before they attacked. This seemed to show that it was a planned attack on me, not a random act of robbery on three strangers.

Matthew, under close questioning, remembered a patch of red hair between the hat and cloth mask on one of them. He also remembered a Scotch accent.

Mary at first made no answer to the questions, merely shaking her head. It was easy to see that the shock for her had been very great. But the chancellor, strangely gentle for so strong a man, persisted with his questions, and she finally said, 'Of course there was the squint.' On this her memory became so vivid that she broke down and could say no more.

After we had been questioned, Matthew, Mary and I were asked to sit on a bench at the side of the hall and he sent for Baldwin's brother, a tall thin man, like Baldwin, but with a nervous air, fidgety. He took the oath.

The chancellor, now erect and strong, his chin raised, went straight in. 'On Sunday afternoon, four men met at your ale-house, sometime after noon. I want to know their names. One had red hair, and one a squint. Another was a Scot. One tall, the others of medium height.'

Baldwin's brother was taken aback. He had glanced at me as he entered and perhaps was prepared for general questions but not for this sudden direct attack.

'The ale-house was very full on Sunday,' he said in a low voice. 'The minstrels from Durham were performing on the green and we had many extra in the house.'

'Perhaps so,' replied the chancellor, evenly; 'tell me, however, about the four men.'

The way Baldwin's brother hesitated while he sought for the least harmful answer could be seen by all. It was the law that no man could remain silent under questioning in a court under pain of torture. An honest innkeeper should have had no difficulty in recalling four men as distinctive as our attackers, even in a large crowd, and if he denied seeing them he might be thought to have been in league with them. Of course, this assumed that the four men had really met up in the ale-house after the attack but the chancellor had already made up his mind about this and was prepared to press home his attack.

It was at this point that Mary whispered loudly to me, 'He has a squint!' which the chancellor, very alert, picked up immediately and said to Baldwin's brother, 'Before you do, tell me, have you had that squint all your life?'

Baldwin's brother, knowing he was recognised, hung his head without speaking.

'Take him away!' exclaimed the chancellor. 'Guard him well.' 'Bring in Baldwin.'

When Baldwin had been sworn, the chancellor looked straight at him and said, 'Your younger brother lead an attack on these three people, mainly to injure the man Edwin. If you know anything you must speak out immediately.'

'I know nothing about it, sir,' replied Baldwin. 'My brother is much younger than me, in fact I brought him up after our father had died.'

'I know that,' replied the chancellor, 'but why has he done this evil thing to these people?'

Baldwin was silent for a full minute while the chancellor waited without moving, then he said, 'My brother believes he owes me a great deal and perhaps he was seeking to punish the man Edwin because of what I told him on Saturday.'

'What did you tell him on Saturday?' asked the chancellor.

'I told him about the bishop coming, about how I had been made to let my prisoners go.' He paused to think, wondering how much to tell us. 'My brother has always had a great liking for me and as we talked we became very angry. Finally, he rushed out shouting that someone would be made to pay for this. I have to tell you that his temper has always been very fierce and we have all learned to avoid him when he is in a rage.'

'Did you mention Edwin, the soldier?' asked the chancellor.

'I told him about the soldier with the hook who had started all the trouble and who had escaped from the dungeon to carry tales to the archbishop.'

The chancellor, now sure of his ground, said, 'It only remains to find out who the other three attackers were; have you any suggestions, Baldwin?'

Baldwin, as white as parchment, replied, 'I will find out their names from my brother, sir, if you will deal leniently with him.'

The chancellor's reply was very stern: 'Bring me their names, without any bargaining. Justice will be done fairly.'

Then he sat back and considered for a few minutes before saying, 'Baldwin you will no longer act as steward on this estate. Until I can talk to your high master you will confine yourself to your room in the castle. To take your place I am appointing two men to work closely together in the post. One of these will be Edwin the soldier who has impressed me with his bearing and persistence. He has asked for my help – now I demand his for a time. The second will be my scribe, Alwed, who has been with us at this table. It will be for Edwin and Alwed not only to rule this estate until new arrangements can be made by the earl, but for them to make a proper record of all the workings of the estate, including the rents due from each tenant.'

You will understand that I was astonished by the chancellor's demand but I had managed small castles, at least three times, in the rear of the duke's army and there was a challenge here which interested me. I looked at Alwed who returned my gaze stolidly. The pay turned out to be twice the pay I would have got as a carpenter but there remained the agreement I already had with Matthew for the summer.

'Sire,' I replied, 'I shall be very glad to carry out your orders but there is a problem; for I gave a promise already to this good man Matthew, who is in dire need of help on his farm, to help him during this summer.' I explained further what we had agreed.

The chancellor frowned and then his face cleared. 'There is nothing here which cannot be rearranged to everybody's advantage,' he remarked. 'You, Edwin, will live in the castle with everything provided on top of your pay, but a quarter of your pay will be given to Matthew. As well as this, I will release Matthew from his estate duties for six months.' And, although I was not sure that this was exactly to my advantage, it would give me Matthew as a good friend outside the castle, and I might have need of friends in the months to come.

I thanked the chancellor and asked that he would make the new arrangements clear to De Bentley and he said he intended to make this his next task. I asked about a room in the castle and he replied dryly that as I was now in charge I should not find this too difficult. He asked me to arrange a gathering of all the staff and tenants in the great hall as soon as possible so that he could explain the changes. He thought that it would be six months before a new steward could be found.

CHAPTER NINE

Looking After De Bentley's Manor

Alwed worked at York in the preceptor's office, having finished his training at Laon six years before. While at Laon he learned the abacus and a small one in a cloth case went with him everywhere. He could move its counters too fast for the eye to follow. He was short, with a thick body, solid and strong. And though his face was thin and starved-looking, his hunger was seldom for food, but for facts, precise and true, on which he could work his arithmetic and write about on his parchments. We got to know each other well and I came to like his skills and strengths as he did mine. I was impatient at first with the way he wrestled with the facts but soon saw that his methods were much better than my own snap judgements and quick decisions, which a life of soldiering tempted me to use, for the work we had to do that summer.

We found that not one of the agreements on the estate was in writing, not even the main tenancy agreements. De Bentley had carried all the arrangements in his head since he took over the manor for the earl some twenty-five years before, and since then the earl's officers had not had the time to travel so far north to record the different agreements and arrangements.

After a long talk with De Bentley, not a well man but who we managed to catch sober, we were able to set down the main features of the estate before looking at all the details.

The whole of the estate was just over five hides, with some four hides kept as the home farm.

Four of the tenant farms were nearly one virgate each and the fifth, Paris's, was half a virgate. Thirty two people worked from the Manor House – most living in their own homes in the village – ten being field workers and the others manor officers and servants, including the sheriff and his three men.

A tumbledown castle made of stone and timber (all the timber had rotted) stood by the side of the manor house. A lean-to at the side was used to store firewood. The village of Panton was a quarter of a mile down the road from the Manor House and had just over a hundred people, over half being children too young to work. There were eight poor-looking cottages, slate roofed, and ten or more tumbledown wattle and daub shacks with grass roofs. Most of the cottages had a good-sized patch of land for cabbages and chickens and one or two were fattening piglets.

The small, squarely-built church, made of stone, lay on the east side of the road between the castle and the village. It had been built round a chapel that had existed in long-forgotten times and it had the only graveyard for miles around.

One of the bigger shacks, with a brick chimney, was the blacksmith's shop, the smith's name being Thomas. His assistant was a skinny, bent old man called Adam. Their constant problem was getting iron to make their wares and they had to make journeys, perhaps four times a year, to the iron smelters in Northumbria. Their stories of these journeys, which they made whatever the state of the country, with a heavy cart and two bullocks, got them many a beer in the ale-house. They had made themselves strange weapons, the strangest of all which while looking like a thick spear, sprung open and wrapped thin arms of iron round the man it hit. Adam would show a scar near his eye made by one of its long fingers when a test went wrong. They told the story at least once a week of how Adam, when younger, had used it against an attacker on the Durham road – who had died of shock!

Adam became a great liar after an hour in the ale-house. Sometimes the one who had died was 'a great red-headed Dane', and sometimes 'a hairy slave, in rags, on the run'. Thomas listened quietly as Adam rambled on and seldom spoke. When they were away fetching iron, Thomas's old father was able to carry out some work with the help of another old villager. In normal times, when Thomas was working, these two old men could often be seen sitting on a makeshift bench as near to the forge fire as they could get.

One of the cottages was the ale-house, kept by Joseph Deroi. A young woman from the village helped him at night when he often had a number of travellers staying in the loft. He made his own ale, which was well spoken of for its strength and taste.

The butcher's shop, where I had been arrested by the sheriff when I tried to sell the dead bullock, was owned by John of Lyn, and the young assistant I had seen that day was called Mark.

The map of the whole estate which Alwed drew at the end of our questionings remains clear in my mind and, before our talk today (you must remember that Edwin was talking to the old priest who set down these notes), I set out a copy of what Alwed drew for you to see.

A glance at my sketch will show that the five tenant farms were arranged west and south of the manor house with the home farm land (not shown on the map), being to the north-east. The River Derwent, flowing to the Humber, ran south-west, separating Malon farm from the rest of the estate.

The land was all low-lying and inclined to flood in winter.

Matthew's farm was called Hartop and he lived there with his wife Mary and their son, John. Hartop was Mary's family home; she had been born there. She was an only child and her mother had died when she was twelve. She married Matthew when she was nineteen and he came to live at Hartop. After two years her father died and they were granted the tenancy. Mary's father had been a travelling carpenter who found enough work on the De Bentley Estate to make him settle there and after a time he was allowed to have the tenancy of Hartop, which had been part of the home farm before that. Matthew had been born in Panton and had been an apprentice

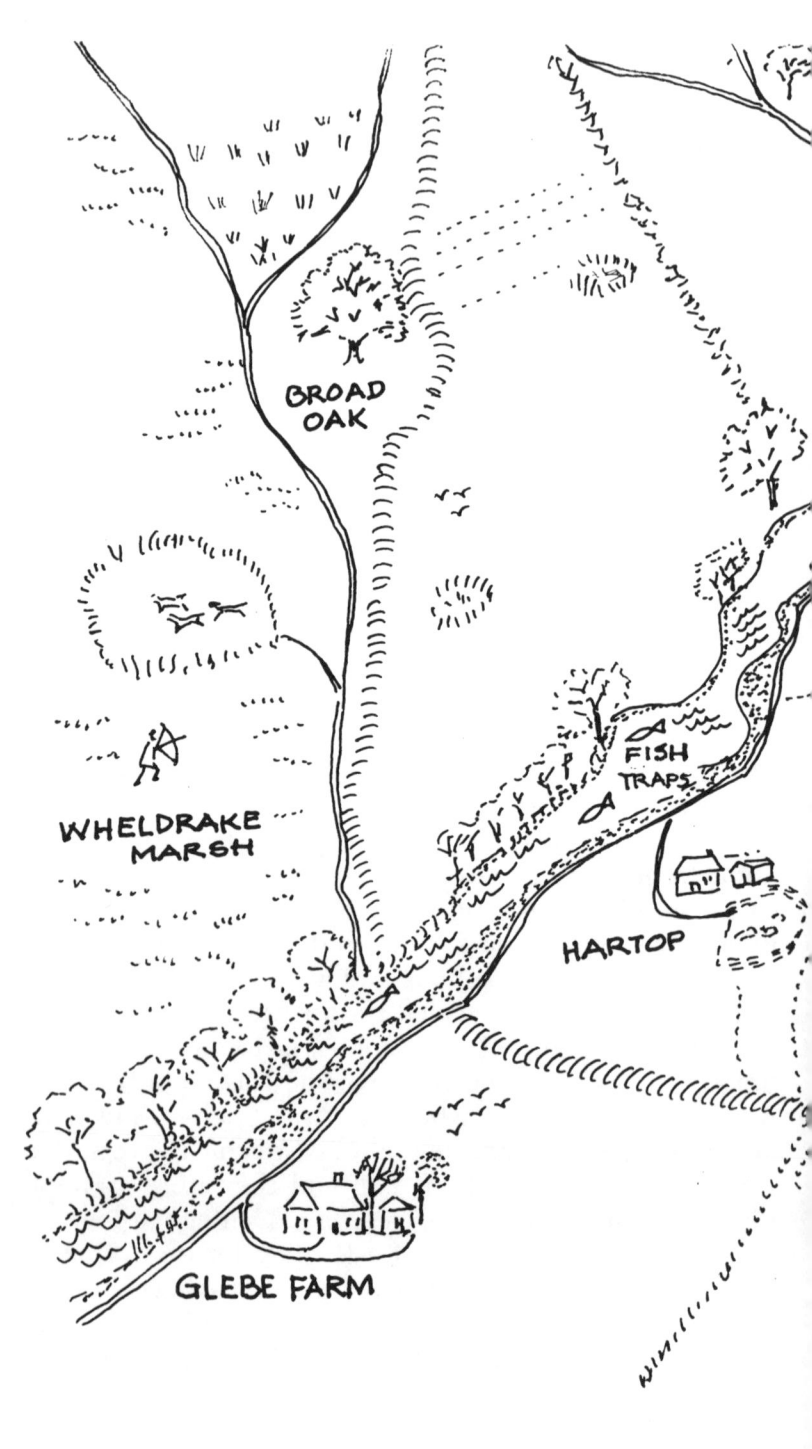

BROAD
OAK

WHELDRAKE
MARSH

FISH
TRAPS

HARTOP

GLEBE FARM

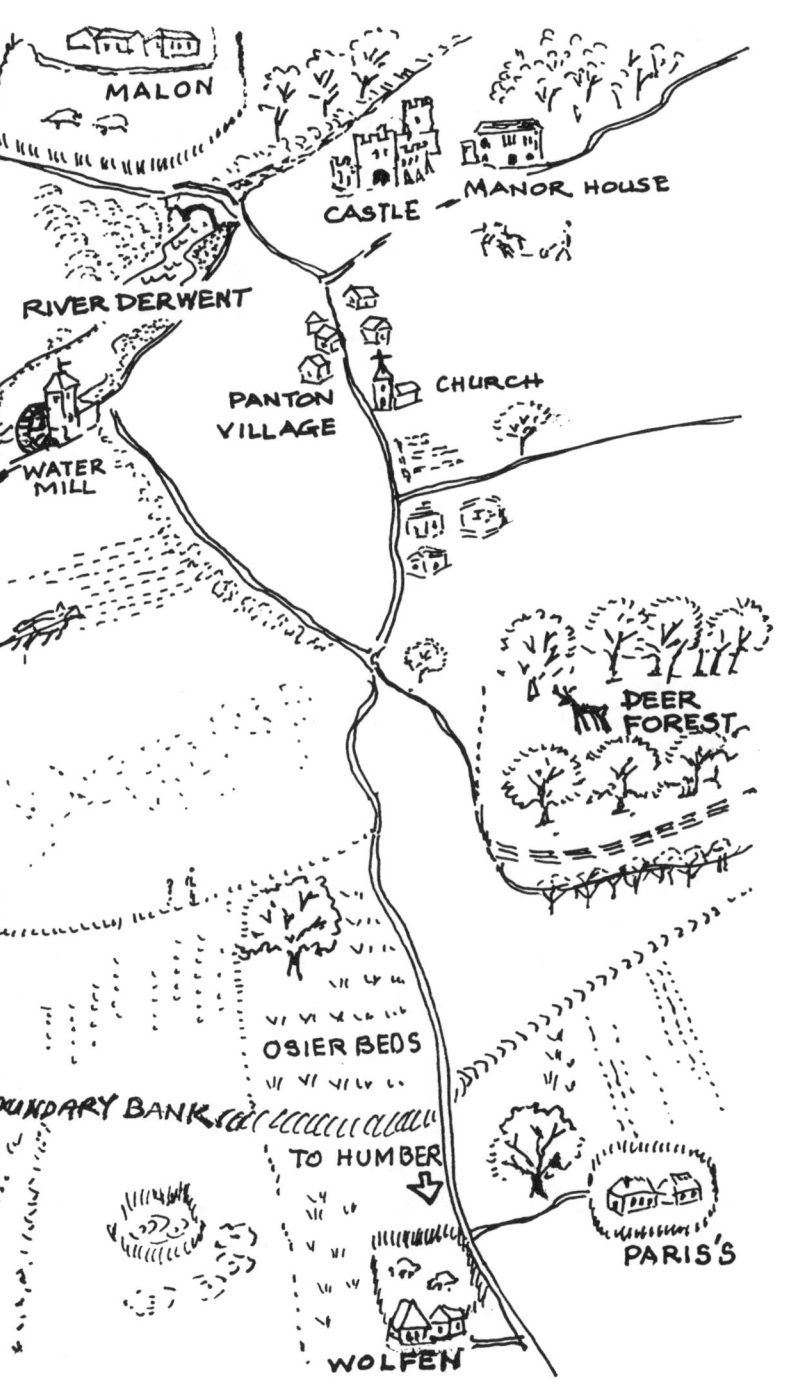

to Mary's father. We asked Mary first about the rent that they paid to the estate.

'When we started,' Mary said, 'the estate gave us three cows and two pigs. From these, we had to give the estate five piglets and ten large cheeses each year. We usually produce as much as this again for our own use or to sell. If we ever leave we must give the estate back three cows and two pigs. And, as well as this, we must somehow find for them fifty planks each year – this was part of the bargain with Mary's father when he stopped being a full-time carpenter on the estate where a big part of his job had been to prepare planks for building repairs.'

'And of course Matthew has to be a carpenter for them for two days each week, throughout the year.'

We asked what other produce they got from the farm.

'We plough for barley, peas and cabbages,' she said, 'and we are allowed to put two eel traps in the river. John runs the eel traps as his own business now.'

It came out that Matthew borrowed the plough from the estate, with their oxen, and had to pay a quarter of his plough crops in return.

Mary continued, 'We have had to argue a lot with Baldwin over the years about the rent due from the plough. It is not easy to decide on what is a quarter of a crop of peas, harvested gradually over a whole month.'

At this point Alwed asked, 'What do you pay them in coin?'

Mary replied, 'We give them no coin but Baldwin has been talking about charging us coin for the plough next year, because the part of our plough crop due to them was so difficult to decide. Twenty pence each day was mentioned as a charge for the plough and team, Matthew working the plough himself.'

'If a cow or pig dies, do you still have to replace it?' asked Alwed, and Mary confirmed that they did. 'Exactly what kind of cow?' asked Alwed, and so the questioning started and went on for most of one afternoon, covering such things as, 'What kind of cheese and how big were the cheeses?'; 'Had the piglets to be of a particular size?'; 'Were the planks of softwood or hardwood?'; and many many more. Finally, Alwed said he had got it all down and that what we must do now was to check it with De Bentley.

The farm called Malon was in the tenancy of two brothers, Reginald and David of Claven. Their old mother kept house for them. Two men from the village carried out most of the farming tasks while the brothers spent nearly all the time they were at home making clogs, at a bench in a workshop at the end of the house. There were a lot of beehives in a strongly hurdled enclosure behind the house.

The brothers' annual rent was thirty pounds of honey, twenty pairs of clogs, and twenty fat geese, and they worked on the estate itself for two days each week, mainly in the deer park. Their father had been the clogmaker in the village and they had gone off to the wars with De Bentley when they were very young. When they came back, they found their father had died and managed to persuade De Bentley to give them Malon, a poor farm, but from which they managed to make a living. The geese flock of twenty birds was lent to them by the estate: in other words if they left the farm they would have to hand the flock back to the estate. They said that they usually managed to get twenty to thirty geese for themselves each year from the breeding flock.

The thick white soles of the clogs were carved from block of wood, usually wood from the alder trees, which in places lined the river and the deep ditches. It was one of their complaints that their own river-bank had few alders and that they had to buy alder wood from other farms on the river. They had a little two-wheeled cart drawn by a bad-tempered mule, and every month they drove to a tannery in York to pick up leather for the clog uppers, often taking finished clogs with them to sell in York.

The deer park was an old idea of De Bentley's, that he had been working on since he was a young and idle squire. The park was about a hundred acres, fully treed, mature trees covering much of the park with hazel planted between them for deer food. They said it had four large lawns. It was well fenced with high hurdles and contained a herd of thirty fallow deer. What I had learned in the New Forest was enough to tell me that the two brothers were skilled in the farming of deer.

Their old mother looked after the house and outside the house looked after the beehives and geese. They said that she was able to talk to bees better than anyone else on the estate.

Just as we had questioned the tenants at Hartop and Malon, so we did also at Glebe Farm, Paris's and Wolfen.

Glebe paid one cloth length and two cheeses, and while this was a light rent, the tenant, Ralph Galton, had to help on the estate for two days each week and provide his own four-wheel cart and two bullocks for these days.

Paris's rent was ten sacks of flour and Adam Paris, the tenant had to work on the estate for three days a week in the ploughing season and provide his own plough and bullocks.

When we got back to the castle after talking to the Craven brothers Alwed was very quiet and seemed to be collecting his thoughts. 'Write it all down,' I suggested, trying to get things moving, but all he would say was, 'Wait a bit.'

Then, while shuffling through a pile of parchments, he told me what was in his mind.

'Ranuld Flamard,' he said, 'set a pattern when he was at Durham which every clerk would do well to copy. Although, being a good administrator, his rules insist on great accuracy in detail, his special trick, which we all now use, was to tie a label showing money-value to every single thing, so that control can be exercised by applying our well-developed arithmetic. It was the phrase about applying arithmetic for which he became famous.'

'And the thing that Flamard wished to compare, in the end, was the yield, or rendering (of a farm or an estate or a mill or a goose) compared to its total resource value.'

Alwed let me think about that for a minute or two. The word 'yield' was new and I asked what it meant.

'Yield is that which is left when all other expenses are paid,' he explained. 'Normally it is the rent paid by a tenant to a landlord, or by the lord of an estate to the King.'

Then he said, 'All today and yesterday we have been talking about geese and planks and honey and we have no way of comparing them to see who is paying too little and who is paying too much rent.'

Again he paused, and I saw that proper accounts for De Bentley's Estate were about to be rendered, for the first time!

He proceeded, 'Flamard used to say that every single thing must be listed and that it must be listed with its value shown in money. Men, rivers, roads, land, forests, deer, soldiers, horses and bullocks and, of course, geese.' (He had a dry sense of humour. The geese had been frighteningly aggressive to us as we looked them over – they could not have had a high value, however it was expressed, in his mind at that moment!) 'However difficult (and Flamard knew that it could be very tedious and difficult), everything had to be first found, its owner established, and then valued and listed.'

Alwed had with him a list of Flamard's values for most common things and said that our task was nothing less than to value and list every single thing on the estate! Only when that had been done would it be possible to make judgements about the way the estate had set its rents to the different farms and houses.

The following five weeks remain branded clearly in my mind because of the way that Alwed and I, throughout each day, raked through everything we could find on that estate, both of us gathering the facts during each long spring day (it was a beautiful spring), and then sitting down after a quick meal at night to make a record of every item we had come across. In those five weeks we got through more candles than most castles use in a year and my eyes were sore with watching Alwed scribble away into the night with an occasional question to keep me awake.

For example, Alwed would say things like, 'A goose is worth a groat, but this is for a normal, ready for the pot, nine month old goose. For old tough geese I take off a quarter so that the goose is only worth three pence, and for one that is heavy and overweight I add a quarter. I have no guidance from Flamard, what do you think, mon ami?'

And I would rub my eyes and scratch my head, and might reply, 'Some of the geese I saw were only fit for fox food!' And he replied, 'Tres bien. Merci. Combien?'

He would sometimes do my count again himself, but mostly he wrote rough notes of what I said, which we used when we sat in the little office at the manor at night, writing up the tallies.

So with all the live and dead things on each farm, and on the Home Farm, each was given a value which almost always related to Flamard's list.

The water-mill gave us the most trouble because we had no guidance from Flamard. We argued for a whole morning about what was a good water-mill and that night, as we sat down with our candles to write up the report, Alwed said, 'I think the way they use the water-mill is the main thing wrong with the estate; it is by no means busy enough. Tomorrow you must go round the farms and find out how much hand-milling is going on.'

Next day I went to Matthew's farm first. He was not very friendly. 'More questions, I suppose,' he said, and when I replied, 'It is hand-mills this time,' he became silent, not answering.

I had to press him. 'Matthew, we have to get back to the water-mill, for grinding. All these little mills are wasteful and against the law.'

He grunted and shuffled. He had strong feelings about the water-mill.

After a bit he said, 'The water-mill costs us a lot of money and we have time to mill our own, anyway. Besides, I have to carry all the corn to the mill, which takes up a lot of time when I could be in the fields.'

I could see he still had something on his mind, and waited for it. 'The miller takes more than his share, and how can we argue!' he said, almost shouting now.

Instead of going to the other farms straight away, I went to the mill.

The miller was sitting on the step of his loading door, basking in the sunshine. His name was Pierre, he had learnt his milling in Normandy, outside Rouen. He was old, a philosopher, certainly a rogue like most millers.

There was plenty of water in the river to turn the mill wheel but the wheel was not turning.

'Short of work?' I asked Pierre.

'Had nothing all week,' he replied.

I sat down by his side. 'Tell me why there is no work for a mill, on this large estate,' I said.

His reply was long, his words slow and deliberate. He had had a long time to think it out.

He put most of the blame on the old machinery in the mill, which broke down regularly, and also the poor way it was repaired by the archbishop's millwrights, who were always slow in coming, anyway. 'When they bring their grain, sometimes they have to wait two or three weeks because of breakdowns,' he said.

And he knew of hand-mills on four of the farms; some of them worked at night so that they could not be seen. One even had a mule mill, hidden in a shed behind the house.

'A water-mill needs to grind five thousand marks of grain each year. This mill grinds two thousand. For a properly run mill, the estate should get about five hundred pounds a year for its share of the fees. This estate gets nothing, after it pays for repairs and my wages.'

We talked for several hours. At the end I thought I knew why Bentley's Estate was so short of money and that night told Alwed.

Every large estate relied very largely on the income from tenants, even when the Home Farm was a large one. This income came in a number of ways as I have told about the tenants on Bentley's Estate - produce of various kinds, help, on so many days a week, the renting of ploughs and tools, and free grazing for estate animals being the main ways.

All these ways produced unreliable incomes. Help from a tenant was seldom given willingly. Tenants worked hard on their own farms and had little energy left to work on the home farm. Produce could only be given if it materialised, and often weather or blight or illness (in the case of animals) prevented this.

A tax on food gave a much more reliable and higher income as all people had to eat, and the best way of doing this was to compel all tenants to have their grain ground in the manor mill and then deduct a regular part for the estate. Grain was more than nine-tenths of the food of the people so that this gave a certain and very regular income for the estate.

However, if the people could use hand-mills to grind flour, this income disappeared and this was why a law that all grain had to be ground in the estate mill was in force in most manors.

De Bentley's long illness, and the loss of discipline that followed, had led to hand-milling reappearing in a big way on his estate so that a large part of his income had disappeared.

A threat of heavy fines and surprise visits by the sheriff soon got the mill going again at full capacity.

Alwed at first insisted on trying to find out the size of each tenant farm but when we came to measure the area of the first farm, which was Matthew's, it was clear that we had no tools to make any new measurements, and we had to rely on the figure which had been agreed by the manor and the tenant, together with our common-sense. Alwed told me that the very old measure, the hide, was a good example of the yield deciding the resource. I did not understand him but he said he would explain later.

Certainly, it was known to everyone that the hide, as a measure, depended on the fertility of the soil, poor soil being collected into larger hides than rich soil. Under the old danegeld each hide, poor or rich, yielded exactly two shillings' tax.

We argued most about those things that were very old, broken hurdles and gates, worn harnesses, bowed walls, potholed roads. We could never agree and could see no way of reaching a precise value for such things. In the end we often each thought of a value and then split the difference.

After a while I could see that Alwed was not just using Flamard's ideas but was trying to add to them. 'A resource must render,' he would say whenever we got stuck, or sometimes, 'What is rendered might measure the resource.'

He sometimes stamped up and down on the sanded floor saying these and similar things and ever since, when I hear hard boots grinding sand on a hard floor, I think of those long days in that little room at the manor with Alwed striding up and down, briskly and as well as he could in three or four yards. I can also remember the prince, before Pont Dracon, stamping up and down in his war tent (I was sentry at the door), saying time after time, 'Will he attack round the wood or through it?' For an hour the prince did nothing else, but at the end he seemed to have an answer, for he gave exact orders for the battle.

In three or four weeks we had written down and given a monetary value to everything at the tenant farms and were about to go to the Home Farm when I noticed that Alwed was adding another question to his usual list of, 'What is the resource?'; 'what is it worth?'; 'what does it yield?' This question was, 'And who is the owner?' And then he would sometimes add, 'A resource owes its owner a yield related to its value,' to tie everything together.

I was able to understand the first two questions, 'What is the resource?' and 'what is its value?' The word 'resource' was difficult for me and I once said to Alwed, 'Does it just mean 'thing'?' and he said, 'Not quite, but you can think of it like that if you like,' and so I did.

The word 'value' I took to be the money I was likely to get for the 'thing' if I tried to sell it.

But I found that many things only had a value if sold with other things. Matthew's privy was not a thing I was likely to be able to sell by itself but it did add to the value of his cottage.

'Yield' I got down to 'rent' after saying to Alwed, 'If I lent the 'thing' to someone, 'yield' is the rent I should ask for?' He grunted, but did not say no.

But 'ownership' was something we both found too difficult. In the end we changed it to, 'Who claims ownership of the thing?' and let others afterwards decide who was the real owner.

To show the kind of problem we came across with ownership, take the geese on Matthew's farm where we had to ask whether they belonged to Matthew or the estate, bearing in mind that they had to be given back to the estate if Matthew left the farm. And however that question was answered, when did the goslings, or some of them, belong to the estate?

For myself, I had spent my life with few things I was able to call my own. As a soldier, I only had things that might be carried in a small pack such as flint and tinder, small clothes, occasional trinkets, and from time to time a little money. After a big fight, some plunder might came my way but this was soon sold or lost, usually at cards. I can remember two pieces which I tried to keep, one a heavy medal with red jewels and enamel, on a heavy gold chain, which I had wrenched from the neck of an Italian knight at Tinchebraie, (all those years ago!); and another a thin parchment book, filled with blue and gold pictures of some Indian religion, which I took out of the breast pocket of a wounded sailor when we stormed a large Moorish ship lying at the quayside in Marseilles.

The medal was stolen by a comrade when he deserted one night when I was on sentry. The parchment book was lost, with the rest of my kit, when we had to run and hide from a troop of horse near the Spanish border, the time we were loaned to the Duke of Burgundy.

It was after five weeks of this kind of work that De Bentley asked us to see him and we climbed up to his room late in one afternoon. He still looked ill and was sitting in front of a large log fire although the day was warm.

He was not polite. 'You men were made into bailiffs, for the summer, by the Bishop of York. You have had no experience and the estate is slowly dying while you take up people's time with clerkly questions'.

I asked what he found fault with, in particular.

'We have not enough food to last out the week. These logs are the last in the wood shed. I have no coin to send to the duke at the end of the month.' He paused, and looked at us. ' Is that enough?' he said angrily.

Late spring is always a hard time for these farming estates. Much goes out, little comes in and nothing is left from the winter supplies. The utmost pressure is needed on all those who can produce, at that time, if hunger and hardship are to be avoided. The tenants do as much as they are able on their own farms and the effort they give to the Home Farm and the estate is not great. Alwed and I had been so concerned with our parchments that we had done nothing to bring in the different rents from the tenants and had not set the Home Farm workers on that work, such as wood cutting, which would bring in produce.

I looked at Alwed, who was deeply hurt. His clerkly skills told him that orderliness led to success. He was working on a grand plan and could do nothing without it, even though the manor house was getting nothing to keep it going. I knew straight away that he could see his fault, he was probably the cleverest man I have ever worked with, but I knew he would find it hard to come at the problem in any other way.

De Bentley gazed at the two of us. He was in a difficult position, with little authority for the time being, ill, and without his old bailiff. He tried a thought: 'Why don't you split the job?' he suggested; 'Let Alwed carry on with his task of setting everything down on his parchments, while you Edwin run the estate so that we can all stay alive!'

He was generous with his offer, two hundredths of everything I collected, in coin, as well as my five pence a day.

I would need his help, and said so, because the agreements had been made by him and none put onto parchment. He replied that he would like to help and that he was feeling better and wanted more to do. He told me to come and see him each morning to talk about the day before and to plan the day.

So I became a rent collector and manager of the Home Farm and never have I had to be so guileful and forceful, not even when I was the head doer for the prince's household in Rheims after the plague had wiped out his household and he had only soldiers to run his big palace.

On the first morning we talked about Matthew's farm and agreed that little could be demanded because of Matthew's long imprisonment. I thought that two large piglets in August was possible and that their stock of peas was high for the time of year. We had to agree to try to get the piglets and perhaps a hundredweight of peas.

I caught Matthew just as he was setting off with John to look at the eel traps. When I explained my errand he became angry. 'They take me off my farm for three months at the busiest time of the year and then press for produce,' he shouted. 'I can hardly keep my little family on what we have, let alone keeping De Bentley and his household!'

It was just becoming clear to me that the whole estate was in a parlous state. What exactly would happen if the manor was starved of rents and nothing could be sent to the duke I was not quite sure, but big changes would be made and the present residents were likely to be cleared out.

I put this to Matthew who said, 'It couldn't be any worse!' but it made him think, and he cooled down. 'I found those planks that Baldwin wouldn't have in the shed and had another look at them. They are all right and we could sell them to Jonkins for his new barns.' (Jonkins was Sir Edward Jonkinier, squire of the neighbouring parish.) 'Also we have too many dried peas, and I could let you have a couple of hundredweight.' Also there are a lot of eels in the traps this week – John and I are just going to empty them – we could let you have a couple of sticks.'

He paused: 'The piglets are the most difficult, can we make it one only, in September? I am feeling much stronger, too – I would like to start work on the estate next week, for one day a week to start with.'

And so we agreed and so I told De Bentley next morning.

His fury was that of a sick man, unable to shout but wanting to so badly that he was almost unable to speak. After a while he grunted hoarsely, 'They will all plead poverty, or the weather, or the fowl pest, or the wet winter, or their new babies, or anything they happen to think of. Go back and get twice what he said he could do.

Matthew seemed to know what I had come back for, before I spoke. He had nowhere to go if he had to give up the farm and De Bentley had the whip hand, even to the point where Matthew and his family would go hungry.

'I will double the peas,' he said. 'Although we shall go hungry, and I will give him everything we catch in the traps for the next two weeks.' He thought for a while, even though I had said nothing. 'As for the piglets, I can only promise what will be there, and a litter is only due next month. I will give him two large piglets in November.'

De Bentley did not show any pleasure when I told him, but told me to go next to the Claven brothers and that he would not be satisfied with less than four fully grown geese, the money value of twenty pairs of clogs, ten pounds of honey (or one shilling), and twenty cabbages.

The home farm gave me the most work. It was a time when great efforts had to be made to get good crops later and the hard-working fieldsmen expected to be fed well, for the work was heavy.

I started with wood for the kitchen fires in the manor house. After talking to De Bentley about his deer park, I went and told the Claven brothers to get help from the old men in the village and rake through Wall Wood for dead-fall wood, enough to fill the manor's small woodshed. The Clavens were shaken that I should ask them to take other people into what they had come to think of as their private park but they agreed that there had been serious losses during De Bentley's illness and that only quick action could save the estate. In the longer term, I told them to get enough coppice wood to fill the large woodshed, to be cut before the end of July. Their helpers could take one tenth for their own families.

I also agreed with De Bentley that two good roebucks should be killed before the end of the week and hung in the manor storehouse. Two bowmen, old soldiers of De Bentley's who were employed in the manor house on domestic duties, were told to get their bows out of the armoury and go with the Clavens to kill the deer. The weather was dull, with no wind, and although out of practice, they both killed cleanly, from cover behind trees, as the small herd was driven past them at the south end of Wall Wood.

We also needed pork and I knew that the herd of swine on Home Farm was some fifty-five strong, with six boars. The head swineherd, Ricard, had been a corporal in De Bentley's Company and his assistant was his son, David. They were by nature aggressive men and possessive to the point of violence about their charges. Even De Bentley (so he told me) found it difficult to instruct them in how the herd should be disposed of. He said that they had a name for each pig and treated them like a family. When I told them that I wanted two pigs killed each week for six weeks they became angry and abusive and demanded to see De Bentley. It was at this stage that I began to sympathise with Baldwin, my strong feelings being that both men would be better in the 'jump'. It took me two mornings of shouting and threatening and finally with the sheriff himself standing by my side before I got my way. Even then I had to kill the first pig myself, which was a large old boar, very strong. Getting him to the butcher's shop took three men, one of whom he chased off the road many times. At the butcher's he was so heavy and strong that he had to be thrown and killed on the ground before being lifted onto the block. I had told them that at least three of the old boars should be killed.

We also needed beef but the Home Farm cows were few in number because of an outbreak of foot and mouth two years before. All the oxen were said to be busy harrowing, rolling or carting. I talked to John of Lyn, the butcher, with his assistant Mark listening to every word. He knew exactly what had happened to all the beef on the estate for the last ten years and so was well aware that the manor was short of beef.

'I tell you what I will do,' he said. 'De Bentley has five acres on the river bank to the north-east of the Manor House which he only uses for grazing his great black horse. If he will let me have this grazing for three years, free of charge, so that I can keep my animals there from market, I will pay him now with a small bull calf, slaughtered and jointed.'

De Bentley was not pleased with the offer. 'The grazing is worth three bull calves,' he said, 'but if he will make that two good bull calves I will agree.'

When I put this to John of Lyn he agreed if one calf could be delivered in one month's time and the other before the end of the week, and on this we shook hands.

The baker at the manor house had told me that she was nearly out of corn and peas and that only enough bread was in the cupboard to last three more days. I went to talk to the miller at the water-mill.

'I thought you would be coming to see me,' he said. 'Unless they have started to grind their own corn they must be out of corn at the manor house by this time.'

I asked him how I could get three hundredweight of mixed flour by the end of the week and, of course, he asked in return when could I let him have the corn to grind. I told him that I could let him have a hundredweight of small dried peas but nothing else; I would have to rely on him finding some corn for me, for which I would try to negotiate a payment.

He thought it would be difficult. Many people were in a similar position, most of their corn being used up at this, the end of winter, and nothing due for another two or three months. However he had in the mill house at that time twelve sacks of mixed corn from a farm outside the estate, which he thought might be for sale and would approach the owner if I wished.

In the end we arranged to exchange half of the old boar for six of the sacks of corn and when the baker complained about the quality of the flour I did not know whether to blame the grower or the miller. One thing I do know, the cakes that she produced for the next three weeks were the hardest and most binding I have ever eaten. One of the Claven brothers who was given one during his day in the park told me that I had invented a new way of making clog bottoms.

In ways such as this, really to nobody's satisfaction, I kept the estate going, so that when one of the duke's men arrived from Winchester at the end of July to take over as bailiff we could present him, Alwed and I, with an estate which was working grumpily but steadily and a plan drawn up by Alwed of how the estate might be run in future.

We all went to see De Bentley together and he told the new bailiff (Andrew de Senlis by name) that he had now recovered from his illness and would expect Andrew to work as his bailiff in the normal way. He also said, rather to my dismay, that he had forgiven Baldwin who would now be assistant bailiff, under Andrew. He thanked us for our work and said that the time had come for us to be moving on. I asked permission to stay with Matthew for another month but he would have none of it and I could see that Baldwin had already begun to assert himself, being no friend of mine.

Alwed of course was eager to get back to his scriptorium and as I now had nothing to hold me back I gathered my things, and early next morning set off with him for York. I was nearly five marks better off than when I had gone to try to sell the dead bullock, so felt satisfied with my eventful summer.

CHAPTER TEN

Journey to York; the City in Riot

It was ten miles to York Minster, with the weather pleasant enough for us to linger if we saw anything of interest, and before long we arrived at the old Viking road from Humber to York.

Alwed had lived in York when he was a boy and as we walked along he told me tales of the Viking attacks, seventy years before, as told by his grandfather who farmed near York. He was a bit of a mimic and he told me how his grandfather told the tale, his voice changing to the voice of an elderly Yorkshire farmer.

'The Danes came for loot, little one (so he called me, interjected Alwed in his normal voice) as they always did. Stories had reached them of the treasure that the Normans had won from taxes and seizures from every part of Yorkshire and they found it a challenge and an affront! After all the Danes had had many friends in the endless acres north of Humber for centuries.

'The straggling crews, after landing in Humber estuary, took carts and bullocks and moved up this very road, sure that there would be treasure for the bringing back.

'When they did come back they had fifty laden carts as well as what they carried. As they marched, they shouted and howled in their strange way. One would suddenly shout something like, "Going to see my granny!" and all the others would howl, "Ow-ow-ow-ow-ow!" Sometimes the shout would not be so nice, but the howl it brought was always the same.

'It was like this with the Vikings. They had been coming, in small parties and large, for centuries, and some had settled on the farms and villages so that they had relations everywhere. They were always easy in Yorkshire, quite at home. Perhaps the granny shouter really did have a granny in York but, if he didn't, some one else with him certainly did. In dealing with the local people, they were always fair, paying for what they took, generously, to get their support. In both the big raids, they stayed in York for only four days and then got out with their loot. It was their way, when they had taken treasure to get back to their ships and home. Plunder was what they lived for, not the hard work of ruling a strange city. Plunder was what made them fight and when they had got it they couldn't wait to get back to their people.'

'They had English allies, landless lords with few men who hoped to ride to power on the back of the Vikings. Earl Waltheof was the best, tall and strong, like his father Siward the Strong, but even he was useless without a following. This was in the '69 raid and they said that Waltheof slew a whole file of Normans as they came, one by one, through a narrow gate.

'Waltheof was well treated by William, but then in '75 he betrayed the King by plotting with the Danes and was beheaded. That was the last Danish raid in these parts.'

In this way, Alwed mimicked the tale of his grandfather.

Soon after we had reached the old Viking road we decided to look at a big windmill which was working a short way off the road, to the north. It was a lot bigger than 'Little Giant' and mounted on a large mound to catch the wind in what was very flat country.

As we went to walk across, three big dogs came barking and we were glad to get back onto the road. Millers are solitaries, hating visitors and others who might hamper their work. They have to pay close attention to the wind outside, in case of gusts or sudden changes, and at the same time watch the grain feeders and the millstones, often in a bad light. It is not surprising that they are tetchy with outsiders.

The dogs left us alone as we jumped the ditch onto the road and we stood and looked at them and the mill, wondering whether to try again. Then a two-wheeled cart, heavy with sacks of grain, came along the road and started to turn into the mill lane and the driver leaned over and asked, 'Has't been chased bi dogs?' and he offered us a ride, explaining that the dogs let carts in but always ran at walkers.

As we came to the front of the sack shed, the carter yelled, 'Heigh Jap,' and a muffled shout came from the buck. The mill was turning much faster than Little Giant and the noise was threatening, a mixture of clatter, rumble, and shudder.

We helped to unload the bags into the shed, and, when they were all in, the miller, who had been watching from a little window near the stones, climbed down to mark the pile of sacks, using withies with signs scratched into the bark.

After this he turned to us, anxious to be back: 'There's only the lad in there,' nodding to the buck; 'I have to get in again.' We could all see that something had to be done, as the mill started to go even faster in the sharpening wind, and a heavier judder set in, which we could feel and hear in the shed. 'Have y'r bait and I'll close her down and come and sit by you.' He was ready for a rest and a bit of a crack.

As he hurried back, he limped on his left leg and I had noticed that he had fingers missing from his left hand. He was a tall, strong man, about fifty years old, with a direct gaze, an alert man who seemed to have a quick understanding. He had layers of dust on his cap and clothes and, although the weather was not warm, he was scantily clad.

The carter put a nosebag on his mule and came and sat with us on a rough bench inside the shed. His name was Japhet, but he said he was always called Jay. He worked with his father on a half-hide holding three miles over towards York.

'He runs it too fast,' he told us, talking about the miller and the mill; 'That's how he lost his fingers, trying to grease the pinions without stopping.'

I asked about his limp. 'Born with it,' he said. 'Difficult birth. Couldn't farm or soldier, went into milling. One of the best. A lot come to see him, from all over. Knows about windmills, more than any other. Takes too many risks. Never had a wife,

116

would have been more cautious.' He gave me a piece of his yellow cheese and I chewed it with my hard gritty bread as the great grey sails of the mill slowed and stopped, and I could see that they were made from woven bark, not linen as at Little Giant. In the restful quiet (after that frightening noise and clatter), the miller limped slowly down the ladder and came and sat with us. He had brought a jug of ale and gave us a wet before he took a long swig himself. He slung a sheepskin coat over his shoulders, in the hut it was cool and he had been sweating.

'Takes both of us to stop it if gets going like that,' he explained. 'Had to put water on the brake.'

He knew Alwed and was respectful to him. The mill was owned by the Minster and he visited the scriptorium once or twice a year to talk about his pay, which depended on what he produced. Alwed told him who I was and he looked at me suspiciously. Ex-soldiers, whether sound, wounded or mutilated, are all too often rascals, dangerous and desperate.

Quickly I told him about Little Giant, the problem with the trestle and how I had solved it. He looked at me strangely, without saying anything for a minute, then said, 'Your mill is wrecked.' And after a pause, 'The miller was nearly killed.'

'Jake?' I asked, and he nodded.

'But the trestle was strong,' I cried.

'Maybe so, but it was lightning that did it, one of the worst storms ever.'

'What are they going to do?' I said, thinking of all the work that had gone into it and going so well too.

'Don't know. Lightning's a bad enemy to windmills. What suits for the wind, standing high up, above everything, makes them targets for lightning, which strikes at high things. If they have found a bad place for lightning, they might be better to take it to another place.'

'Have you ever had a lightning strike at Scoreby?'

'We have been lucky so far, one small strike which did no damage. But we will get one sometime! We haven't found a saint yet to speak for windmills!'

I liked the man and wanted to cheer him. I said, 'They say that lightning never strikes twice in the same place.'

'That might be true,' said Jap, 'but they also say, "Once bitten, twice shy." I hear that the nuns don't know whether to repair it or move it.'

I thought straight away that I might alter my plans and go back to help the prioress with whatever she decided, but then I thought again that they had five people there who had made the windmill.

We finished our bait, said goodbye to the miller, and got a lift from Japhet for two miles along the road towards York. We jumped off just before he turned into the lane to his father's farm and we found ourselves walking between small fields with people busy harvesting peas and beans and parsnips, the corn in some of the fields not yet properly ripe. They seemed friendly people, one or two waved, another gave us a 'Good-day'. The road to York was straight ahead and after a while we saw horsemen approaching, a small troop, I thought about six or seven. Soon we saw that they were horse soldiers, riding at ease, slack and untidy.

One, with a bloated face and no cap pushed his horse forward, pulling at it to make it rear over us, and shouted, 'What are you?'

We dodged the horse as it came down but stood firm. As a servant of Archbishop Tunstall, Alwed had no need to be afraid of any man in that part of the kingdom and I too, in a sense, was in the archbishop's employ.

'We are officers of the archbishop,' said Alwed, 'going to the Minster.'

'Any bloody footpad can say that,' swore the untidy one. 'Show us something.' And a voice from behind him said, 'Money, for choice!' Bloated Face was drunk, as well as untidy. 'You look like a deserter,' (in my direction); 'And you like an runaway clerk,' (to Alwed). 'You there,' pointing at me, 'which Company hast'a run from?'

I had led too many patrols myself on this kind of work to fall into any of the traps. If we were to start to fumble for badges or parchments, then they would push us with their horses, knock us down and leave us lying. If we jumped the hedge and ran, they would hunt us down and use us for sword practice.

I stretched to my full height, head raised, and I sensed that Alwed was following my lead. 'Your leader,' I demanded,

118

speaking in the French of authority, as used by the prince, firmly and in a way that made refusal impossible.

My tone made him sit up in the saddle but he was still lost in a drunken haze.

'We—have—no—leader!' he shouted, forming each word as a child might, 'We—need—no—leader!' He took easy to bullying, like most soldiers on horseback, and I knew we might be in trouble. 'Knock 'em, Bart,' said someone behind him, and Bart raised his legs to kick his horse forward to push us down.

Instantly I cried, 'Halt.' A command. My voice (after all those years!) pitched like that which had commanded a hundred men halfway through the great fight at Pon Dracon, when the prince was rallying his battered army and I had been left in charge of the company. Bart hesitated. No more advice came from behind.

'On your way,' I ordered, loudly and firmly into the silence. 'The archbishop's bodyguard follows us, from yonder lane.'

Stories about the archbishop's bodyguard were told all over the kingdom. He was a holy man, too holy those said who paid their dues to Holy Mother Church by political manoeuvring, but, in compensation, his bodyguard was one of the most soldierly in the kingdom, being noted for its strictness and its ruthlessness, as well as a deep loyalty to the archbishop.

By accident, I had hit on the best threat of all. (I only found out later that the leader of the archbishop's bodyguard had soldiered with me for some years in the prince's army.) It took no more than an instant for the band to pull their horses round and kick them into a gallop back along the road to York.

Alwed and I stood, erect and still, in the middle of the road until they were out of sight, and then sat down on a grassy bank. It had been a narrow escape.

A head arose above the hedge, 'Too many about. No bosses, nobody's men.' It was an old field worker, hoeing parsnips, and we talked for a minute or two. Then he showed us a path away from the main road, also leading to York. We were glad to take it.

After going a couple of miles, at the top of a little rise, we saw in the distance the tall white fence which had been built round the burnt-out ruins of the Minster. The town was on our left, with smoke hanging – very peaceful in the afternoon sunshine. But then, as we stood and listened, we started to hear shouts and cries and these soon turned into the loud, angry, rumbling noise of a rioting crowd.

It brought to my mind the noise made by the large mob of peasants in Lyon (they were in revolt against the Prince of Burgundy), as they stormed up the hill to the castle where I was facing them with my troop.

And I knew the din that a mob makes when it is going for blood from a lot of other times too. Something like a million stinging bees swarming out of a thousand smashed hives all looking for someone to hurt. And add to this, usually, the noises of fire crackling, buildings crashing and hundreds of stupid cries and shrieks.

As yet we could see no fires, but the noise, which was great, seemed to be from a large mob.

'It's the discharged soldiers, out for trouble,' I said to Alwed. 'If we run into Bloated Face and his lot they will kill us, after they've played with us.' We stood, worried and uncertain, until Alwed replied, 'It sounds near the castle. If we go across that waste we will get to the Minster without running into them.' The Minster was on the north side of the town with a gate in the side of the new fence, sited away from the town. The waste was part of the desolation left behind by William the Bastard fifty years before and not yet built on.

Part of me wanted to follow Alwed and get to safety, but another part, moved by the instinct of an old soldier, urged me to get nearer to the rioters to find out what was going on. When I told Alwed he shrugged his great shoulders and said, 'Lead on, lad.'

The path we had been on entered a narrow street that was full of potholes and piles of rubbish. All doors were closed and window holes closed up. No one was about. 'Love Lane,' said Alwed as we hopped along it; 'We turn right at the bridge over the river to get to the castle.'

We picked our way to the bridge and from the middle of it could see the mob clearly. It wasn't moving at all but everyone seemed to be watching something that was going on in the middle.

The din and shouting were very loud but it was not the steady roaring of a mob on the attack but came in bursts.

A man and his heavily laden donkey came hurrying over the bridge and we stopped him (He was not willing to stop, I had to grab his halter!), and asked about the meaning of the noise. 'It is the discharged soldiers,' he said. 'They are having sport with four prisoners from King David's army'.

We hurried away along a narrow path leading to the Minster and were soon banging on the gate. On Alwed shouting his name, we were pulled inside and the door firmly bolted again with a six-inch square crossbar. And as I looked round at what was in front of us, I was easier, seeing that I had fallen in with a full company of armed men, well prepared for any kind of trouble.

In what had been the courtyard of the old Minster, the archbishop's bodyguard itself was drawn up in two ranks. They were dismounted and at attention, their horses held by servants to one side. Each man was armed with a lance and a short sword, and wore a steel headpiece and a thick leather jerkin. No man was less than six feet in height and they stood proudly rather then stiffly.

Standing in front of them, giving them their orders in a commanding voice, was a smaller man, similarly dressed but without a lance and with silver spurs at his heels. I knew him straight away, we had been sergeants together under the prince fifteen years before. He was called Robert Weynthorpe and had been one of the hardest drivers in the prince's army. We had been good comrades, opposite in temperament but strong in a common purpose, to serve the prince. Now here he was, Captain of the Archbishop's Bodyguard, one of the most famous body of soldiers in the country.

He was giving his troop their battle orders.

'We think there are five hundred rioters. They have been torturing some Scots prisoners who had been promised freedom and have hanged one of them. Now they have started to loot the shops near the old castle. Hear your orders.' He paused and then went on:

'We will go out of here and circle round the town to come on them from the south.'

At this point there was a stir near the abbey and the archbishop himself came through the doorway and walked

121

towards Weynthorpe, who, when he saw who it was, saluted the archbishop with his short sword. I was near enough to hear all that passed between them.

'Captain,' said the archbishop, 'before we use any force, I would like to address all the rioters and would ask you to have them gathered together on castle hill. I ask you to send the town crier into the town, escorted by a small body of men, to say that I will address them in half an hour on castle hill and that I shall have something to say which most of them will find attractive.'

CHAPTER ELEVEN

The Archbishop's Speech

In the warm evening of that fine August day, the archbishop took up a position on Castle Hill, facing the crowd squarely, like a general of troops. Weynthorpe was at his right hand, a little behind, and because Alwed's presence in the courtyard had been noticed by the archbishop, he had asked him to go with him in case he needed a scribe. Alwed had asked me to go with him and after I had made myself known to Weynthorpe, he readily agreed. We stood on the archbishop's left, Alwed sometimes scratching notes on a parchment.

The setting sun shone directly at us, lighting up the archbishop's scarlet and gold in a way which caught every eye. He held a sceptre in his right hand. The many-colour jewels in his chain and a big yellow-red gem at the top of his mitre flashed and sparkled in the golden light of the setting sun; yet against all this colour his face was quite white because he was still weak from his illness. He had been carried to the castle hill on a litter and before it was taken away he was helped down to face the crowd. He stood quite erect, slight, very still. Somehow quite holy.

The crowd had been pushed into a crescent by his bodyguard with the nearest only twenty paces away. They were standing on the reverse slope of the great trench, facing Castle Hill, so that each one could see the archbishop, and hear him speak, without effort. Ten men of the guard were spaced at the back, splendidly horsed, each lance carrying the archbishop's colours.

He stood for a minute until they were quiet and mannerly, and then spoke slowly and precisely for a quarter of an hour in his fine voice which carried easily in the quiet air. He spoke with high authority and very directly, and none moved after his first words.

He spoke in English, which to men who had only heard high-born persons speak in French, was very striking. I went through Alwed's notes with him the next day and so can well recall how the speech went.

He might have scolded them but he started with a blessing, welcoming them to York, thanking them for fighting so well for the King at the great battle with the Scots. It was well known to them all that the archbishop had himself collected together the King's forces for that great battle, even though he had had to be carried on a litter to Northallerton. It was acknowledged too that he had only with difficulty been stopped from taking a leading part in the battle itself, even when he was weak and ill. Then he went on:

'In my life I have found that even though a man tries hard to find his duty it is seldom that he succeeds, and in fact many men never manage to find their proper duty in this world. And I have seen that most men do not seek too hard, but wait, usually in vain, for a proper duty to offer itself. And it therefore follows that he who is fortunate enough to find a good path must follow it to the end, no matter how rough he might find it.

'Now that your recent soldiering is over, many of you will be wondering how to find your way back to the right path so I want to tell you something about the meaning of "proper path".

'All your actions will in the end be judged by God and we of the church can tell you what will be judged to be good, and what bad. And I want to remind you that no man can go through life without acting badly, probably many times, no matter how hard he might try always to do good. So that if God, in His infinite mercy, is going to allow us to balance our good actions against all our bad ones, we must be very careful, each one of us, to do each good thing which is offered to us by God.

'And it will be on the balance which we strike between good and bad that God will decide where we shall spend our eternity.'

I remember that having got them interested he paused (and they stayed quite still), and then he went on:

'Because you have been in battle you will have deep thoughts about heaven and hell and where you will go to when you die.

'The sight of several thousand men who have died dreadfully, mostly with terrible wounds, is a more certain way of making a man think of the afterlife than any sermon I can give.

'The soul of each of those dead men is now either in heaven or hell, and, depending on how he behaved in life, he will now either be enjoying the glorious pleasures of heaven or writhing miserably in the fires and tortures of hell.

'And because it is certain that we shall die and never certain how long we shall live, we should conduct our lives each day so that our souls will be saved for Heaven, even though we die that night.'

'A wise man has said, "This world is but a thoroughfare and full of woe, and when we depart therefrom, right naught we bear with us but our good deeds and ill." '

I saw men in the little bands that made up the crowd look at each other anxiously. From their own parish priests they were used to more comfort.

Then he put his offer to them.

'Our plans for building a new Minster are well afoot. The old one served us well for a hundred years and it has left us with many beloved memories. The new one will be even bigger and it will be built entirely of stone. A model of it has been made and will be shown to those of you who accept my offer. The main tower will be two hundred feet high. We will use whatever stone we can recover from the old building but, even so, we shall want more than ten thousand cart-loads of stone. For some of the stone for the carved parts, we will have to send to France. The whole will take some twenty million man-days to finish, over some seventy years, and only a small proportion of the men who work on it will see it finished. Most of the builders will only see one part completed, such as a wall or perhaps a large carved doorway.

'And the men who do the work at the start will leave nothing which can be seen. The work they do will be buried with the foundations.

'But all of the work, of whatever kind and whenever done, will count as work on God's house, done for the Glory of God, done for the salvation of mankind. And I will give full absolution to each man who helps me to carry out this work, for all his sins.'

He went on to explain to them that war, in whatever cause, brought much evil in its train. Fortunate indeed was the soldier who did not sin so grievously in war that his chances of entering Heaven were small. The point went home; I saw many heads hang low.

'As well as the absolution,' he went on, 'all workers will be housed and given one good meal each day, with ale. And after a man has worked for one month, pay at the rate of three pence each day will be paid, those elected as foremen being paid double.'

He said that he wanted one hundred of the men in front of him to start work the next day, on those terms. His officers would be present in front of the Minster gate that evening to take the names of those who wished to be considered.

Those for whom work could not be found should come back to where they were now next day in mid-morning, when food would be provided and a blessing given before they departed for their own country. They would be escorted by men of the bodyguard for the first ten miles of their journeys.

He gave them a brief blessing (this time most bowed their heads), and walked down the hill and through the crowd, with Weynthorpe leading the way (and being ready to support him if necessary), with Alwed and I following, back to the Minster. Once inside the white fence, he stopped and turned to the three of us and said, 'Find me one hundred good men from that lot, to stay for three months to clear the site and start digging the foundations. And first they must put up site shelters for themselves and those who will follow. Send out messengers to all our properties, Alwed, to say what building materials are required for the site shelters and to ask them to send them to the Minster without delay.'

The matter of the riot had been forgotten by everybody. I never found out what happened to the four Scots.

Alwed and I first went to the refectory that was in a large house in the town, just outside the white fence. We had not eaten since our talk with the miller at Scoreby and it had been a busy day. One of the porters was in the kitchen, an ugly man who scowled as we entered, other meals having finished long before. However Alwed was known as an officer close to the archbishop and rather surlily we were found some bread and hot mutton stew, together with a jar of ale.

As we were finishing, Weynthorpe came in and roared at the porter, 'Jacko, meat and ale, fast!'

He sat down at our trestle, clearly tired, and said, 'That went well!'

We sat until he finished and I had time to look at him for the first time. He looked a lot older and was very fine in his bodyguard uniform, but I remembered him as a working soldier, dressed practically, in clothes fit for a soldier who might have to fight and sleep and run and swim and climb. I thought I liked him better like that. But he looked strong and I heard later that he drilled his troop, he himself, for three hours every day. We got to talking about the old days and the disaster at Caen soon came up – it was the only time that either of us had run, scared, in a routed army. We had become separated and had not seen each other since.

Afterwards we were too tired to do anything and Alwed found me a litter in one of the refectory rooms before going off to his own quarters. As we parted, he asked me to find him in the scriptorium early next morning so that we could start to recruit our workmen.

CHAPTER TWELVE

Setting the Men to Work

At daylight a queue of men stretched for two hundred paces along the south fence, and, after we had set up a table, the first to come forward was Dexter Roberts. I got to know Dexter well because he was soon made foreman under me.

He was a man of middle age, tall and of great strength, who had come north to join the King's army, from a hamlet on the estate of Marc de Ville in Northamptonshire, with three others, led by Mortain, the squire to Sir Dan Salene. They had joined the great army just three days before the battle, in which Squire Mortain and his three comrades had all been killed when they were cut off from the main force in one corner of the field by a strong body of Scots. Dexter's weapon had been a great axe which had been captured from a Norseman by his grandfather in a Viking raid thirty years before and which had been carefully hidden by the family ever since. After a few weeks, when I knew him better, I got him to draw his axe from the armoury (where all their weapons were stored for as long as they worked on the Minster), to show me how he handled it; the sight of this huge man whirling the large battle axe round his head was very frightening, even to an old soldier like me. It was by wielding his axe in this manner while running at the Scots that he had escaped after his comrades had fallen.

He told me that when he went back the morning after the battle to find Mortain's body amongst the thousands lying in

129

the field, he found that most of the bodies had been stripped of their clothes and other markings by scavengers and, being exhausted, he could find neither the strength nor inclination to turn over hundreds of naked and bloody bodies in a long search.

He said it was a great grief to him that he had not been able to save Mortain's life and he needed the comfort of Archbishop Thurstan's absolution for this, not for the three or four Scots he had managed to kill earlier in the battle.

When I knew him better, I asked him how he, a small-time farmer, had suddenly changed into a soldier, without any training. He said that Squire Mortain had drilled them each evening as they marched to Yorkshire but the greatest persuaders had been a company of Flemish mercenaries drawn up at the rear of the army, put there to prevent anybody from falling back without orders. They had hanged a dozen men on convenient trees to show what happened to those who ran away.

Dave of Patcham (for so Alwed wrote down his name, he only knowing himself as Dave, born in Patcham in the south country) claimed to be a worker in rough stone. 'Not a mason, Master,' he said, 'I has no skill in carving and fine measuring. But give I a large block of sandstone or limestone and I will have it into handleable pieces quicker than any man.' Him I told to go and report to Master Moston, the mason in charge of the south wall.

A man I shall always remember was Pen Hacking, from Blackburnshire. He was a bowman, trained in Bowland Forest to shoot deer for the royal table. He had never shot at men before and it had sickened him. Absolution and a steady job was what he wanted now and he could see that the building of the new cathedral could be a job for many years. His building experience was in rough stone work, field walls and outbuildings.

So we talked to forty-two men (Alwed's records were very complete) that first morning and sent thirty of them off to talk to building masters on the site. The others we sent to the refectory for a meal and told them to attend on the parade ground at noon when the archbishop would give them an absolution in congregation before they left for their homes.

And so it went on for four mornings, the last two in steady rain, so that Alwed was unable to write until we had an ancient campaign tent brought from the armoury. We got a hundred good workers out of that ragged army and fed the rest and sent them home. There was a little jousting and shouting in the town the first night, and we held a mounted troop ready on the parade ground, but they soon settled down and the nights after that were quiet. The rest of us were on short rations for a week until new supplies could be got from the parishes. I had to use the piece of cheese carried from Bentley's kitchen to season many bowls of stewed parsnips before we got back onto our mutton and bacon dishes!

On the fifth morning, Alwed and I visited each of the master masons on the site. As is the way with master masons few of them were very happy with the men we had sent but agreed 'to try them'. In any case it seemed to us a good thing that the men had to regard themselves as being on trial for a time with their new masters.

I saw as we recruited the men that they took particular notice of the way in which Alwed wrote down their names. Few of them had had their names written down before, probably not since their christening by the parish priest, an event that they were unlikely to remember. One of them, a thin weakly looking man with a weasly face asked to be shown his name and looked at it for some time, puzzled.

They were leaderless men. Leaders who had escaped alive from the battle had led their men home, but these men had seen their leaders killed and they had no one to lead them away.

Most were serfs, sent as part of the old feyr offering set up from ancient times to defend the kingdom. A few were freemen, each anxious to defend his home and willing to fight for it and for the booty which might appear. Craftsmen were scarce but we found many who had become rough joiners or stone workers by working on their own farms or those of their masters. All seemed anxious for guidance on what they should do now, when their task for the King was finished, and they were faced with long journeys through the country without leaders to speak for them. Bands of leaderless men were not welcome in any village or manor.

As we were walking back after talking to the masons about their new recruits, we noticed men running and some shouting at the end of the site where the foundations were highest. We ran towards it to find that a tall young man was lying lifeless on the ground with a large block of stone against him. When questioned, the labourers said that the stone block had slipped from its tongs and knocked the man down before rolling to rest. The tongs were still swinging at the end of a rope that passed over a pulley hanging from the top of a three-legs.

There was nothing to be done for the man, a corner of the stone had crushed his head, so I looked carefully, first at the tongs and then at the pulley, which was ten feet above my head.

I could see nothing wrong with the tongs, which were made of strong iron, except that the points needed sharpening, looking up at the pulley I saw at once that it was split and that the rope had fallen onto the axle.

Something I had heard the prince say to a young knight came back to mind. The knight had been asked to find out why so many horses were casting shoes, on the march, and he came back to say that the farrier was sure that it was the state of the roads, which in truth were very soft and muddy. The prince was very tolerant of young men, and he looked at him for a few seconds before saying:

'It is my own experience, and that of all men who have carried out tasks other than the very simplest, that, when something goes wrong, it is not due to one simple cause but almost always due to three causes which have worked together. Thus a badly trained knight will choose a bad spear for the tourney because whoever trained him was himself poorly skilled. So that you have a badly trained knight, a bad spear and a bad trainer, and, while the peasants will blame the spear, the fault lies in three places, not one. Go and find out for me what the other two causes are of the casting of so many shoes.'

I heard from the farrier's assistant that on further questioning the knight found out that the farrier had been given soft nails that were also too short, by a quartermaster who was making money on the side. Thus here also you have three things, the muddy roads, the bad nails and the greedy quartermaster.

As I stood there thinking about the stone, I was puzzled about the third cause, after the broken pulley and the blunt tongs, but one of the labourers, after we had been there for a few minutes (with the dead man still lying next to the block), said, 'It slipped, up top.' Then I saw that the rope holding the pulley had slipped a knot so that there would have been a bad jerk on the lifting rope, which had then broken the pulley and jerked out the tongs. That the pulley was very old was also clear.

Just then the archbishop came up, with Weynthorpe at his elbow, and asked Alwed to explain what had happened. Between us we came out with the explanation of the three things that had gone wrong and the archbishop said loudly, so that all could hear:

'We are having far too many accidents with scaffolding and lifting tackle. I do not think that they are being kept in good repair. Our good masons are so concerned with their geometry and the quality of stone that they leave lifting and such work in unskilled hands.

'Edwin, I hope that you are staying with us for a time, so can I leave you to set up a workshop for scaffolding and lifting tackle, so that all such equipment can be inspected and repaired as frequently as you think is necessary?'

(Alwed told me later that the archbishop had some fear that talk on the site might be that the devil was at work, because of the accidents, and he was taking practical steps to prevent this.)

The archbishop was not a man I could say 'no' to and so I found I had the difficult job of collecting all the rotten poles and ancient ropes, not to speak of the cracked pulleys and rusted iron-work, then getting these into some kind of order so that the unskilled men who used them would escape unhurt. The masons were impatient of delay and I was not popular on the site for some time – not in fact until they saw that the attention we were giving to the equipment involved them in fewer accidents and the long delays that were inevitable after such accidents.

The Master Builder was called Fulk, and everybody called him Master Fulk. Of middle age, he was one of those rare men who are fat and heavily built but at the same time tremendously active. Three senior builders under him were responsible for different parts of the cathedral but he was the only one who understood the overall plan. Even the archbishop, with whom he had daily meetings, was unable to remember all the details because of the heavy pastoral duties which he had to carry out for the whole county of York.

Master Fulk was probably the least religious man who had ever worked on a cathedral. With the archbishop he was very direct, at times nearly blasphemous. I once heard him say, firmly and clearly:

'Your Worship will do well to remember that I am the only man on the site who can build a cathedral that will stand for centuries. Your other helpers either lack my skill or, more frequently, regard the work as a penance which, like all penances, will be better when uncomfortable and hurtful, so that if a piece of a wall falls down, they regard it as God's will that they should suffer a still greater penance by rebuilding it. If I allow myself to work like that, you will never have a cathedral in five hundred years. As your worship knows, most cathedrals either fall down or are burned down. I am capable of building a cathedral which will do neither if you will let me exercise my hard-won skills to make sure that all the penances are used up in useful, long-lasting work, not in those painful failures which surely cannot be pleasing in the eyes of God.'

I had taken Dexter Roberts on as my assistant and one day when we were talking together in a corner of the yard about scrapping some old scaffolding a very angry Master Fulk came up to us and asked us loudly what we thought we were doing.

It ended by Fulk shouting so that the whole yard could hear him that his masons were quite capable of deciding which equipment was safe and which was not and that they didn't need a broken-down soldier to tell them anything.

Within two days I had seen the Archbishop and received his blessing before proceeding on my journey.

Two days later I was walking into Tentwell and the first person I saw was you, yourself, Father Riveaux!

APPENDIX ONE

Father Riveaux's Comments on Royal Deer Forests

Priest: It is essential to remember that the most important purpose of any Royal Forest is to farm deer. In other words, it is a place where deer are husbanded for their meat. Its other important purpose is that of a source of timber, the timber harvested being of a number of types, from small twigs for domestic fires to large oak beams for shipbuilding and building purposes. All has to be skilfully managed, both to produce the biggest 'crops' and to prevent losses by thieves and neighbouring landowners and peasants. Other purposes of the forest include supplying small animals (such as hares) for the benefit of local landowners who usually shoot them themselves, and, also quite often, fuelling forges, which utilise the charcoal made from forest wood. All these functions are a source of income to the King, as is the system of agistment, whereby local farmers are allowed to graze their beasts in the forest, for rent, at certain times of the year.

The word was that deer-killing provided Stephen and his friends with entertainment, particularly when a wounded deer had to be chased through the forest. But they said that neither Rufus nor the first Henry regarded deer killing as anything but a butchering operation, most of the killing being done by driving the deer into an ambush of bowmen who pick off carefully selected deer, with a high chance of a quick kill.

From what I have heard at the eyres I have attended, deer are quite easy to kill. We had a poacher before us when I was juryman who had caught a number of deer by arranging a network of cords with a number of shiny, dangling things in the middle, and deer being curious would put their heads into the snare to examine the shiny things. He said his main problem was to find shiny things of the right weight and size and that he had found that pieces of an old discarded helmet, when polished with sand, served very well. I remember the court could not find out where he got the helmet. He was to have hanged, but died in prison.

Edwin worked for nine months in the forest and, because he was an observant man and had had plenty of time to pick up the forest practices, I asked him to describe some of his experiences. For instance, did he ever meet a royal hunting party?

Edwin: I was never able to see a royal hunt at work. The nearest I got to it was when Hugh asked us to assist in a hunt for which two courtiers of Stephen's had obtained permission, each to kill one hind or doe. (It was November, the stags were weary with rutting and bad tempered if approached.) Six of us tried to drive four fallow hinds and a buck towards the courtiers who were badly hidden behind two willow bushes. This nearly cost Hughy his job when the courtiers complained, back at Winchester. As the deer moved towards the willow bushes, the wind changed and they picked up the very courtly scent of the courtiers. The hinds immediately turned and fled back right past us but the buck, in high dudgeon, put down his massive spade-like antlers and charged the nearest courtier. For a fallow buck, he was a big animal and as we had advised the courtiers to dismount to shoot better, it must have been a terrifying sight to them. Luckily, the one the buck charged flung himself down under the bush and his scream made his companion do the same. The buck then seeing a group of us approaching (making a loud noise, I can tell you!) made off after its band.

But to return to a typical day, I remember very clearly one

on which I learned a great deal by being stormbound in a forest hut with Hugh Torens and John.

John and I had been working since first light to clear the ride alongside the Planey Brook. It was November, cold and raining steadily. The work was hacking away the overhang to make a ride five paces wide for the King's gallop.

I should tell you that it is the usual way with the Royal parties, after the ambush and the killings, to gallop at full speed along a prepared track in the bailiwick in which they have been hunting. This often takes the form of a race so that after the long wait in the ambuscade men and horses are thoroughly exercised and warmed up. If the ride is arranged properly, along the side of the bailiwick, it also serves to drive any deer back into the forest away from the boundary. It is these races which give the peasants the idea that deer-hunting consists of a chase after deer by horsemen.

As we cut them, we dragged the cuttings into clearances about two hundred paces apart along the side away from the brook so that in late winter deer could chew the bark from the thicker branches and eat the thinner shoots. While the forest itself was mainly oak, a ten-year growth of willow and elder overhung the ride, with a thick layer of brambles and low stuff on the ride itself. The hook on my right forearm was better than a hand for pulling out the prickly rough wood and I had a cloth wrapped round the other hand to save it. We were making only slow progress. Two mountain ash trees had fallen across the ride in the gales of October and had to be axed before we could move them.

By noon, being wet and very tired, we were glad when Hugh Torens rode up on his small pony and ordered us to a low shed a quarter of a mile away. There we built a hot little fire and joined Hugh in some oatcakes that he had kept dry in a saddle bag. Then, after we had dried a little, the rain still being heavy, with a strong wind, we set to work in the shed to build some hurdles from a pile of withies brought from outside the shed, and as we worked we talked, as men will do when the work is easy and needs little thought. Once, I remember, I said I was surprised that the King himself took such an interest in the deer forests, and Hugh's answer has stuck firmly in my mind.

'You have to understand,' he said, 'that only a king can plan the future, in this and many other things. We ordinary folks are too much concerned with living through today and few of us would bother to plan our future, even if we were clever enough. With deer, you have to work a long-term plan, and quite a difficult one at that, if the King and his friends are to be still eating venison in ten years time! If such a plan is not made and carried out with much discipline, deer will be killed off in a very few years – they are quite easy to kill – and a valuable source of a most delicious meat will dry up.'

I asked Hugh whether it was not just a matter of guarding the deer and letting them live in peace, but he said that it was much more complicated than that. After a few minutes' thought he said that he could name us four things which were very important in managing deer.

The first was that great care must be taken to kill only selected types of deer, these types being selected by experienced deer managers, and furthermore those carrying out the slaughter should also be familiar with the types to be killed and the ways to recognise them. As an example, he said that stags that are past their prime can certainly be considered, but these should not be killed immediately after the rut when their flesh is valueless. Nor should they be killed in the winter, before they have recovered, but in the early summer when they will be fit for eating. Hinds and does will only be killed when herds have grown too large for the space and food available, so that in a well managed forest there will be a time during which the herd is building up and none are killed.

To kill only the right kind of deer, at the correct time of the year needs a proper plan, with deer being driven slowly and without panic towards skilled hunters who must be given enough time to look at an approaching animal to decide whether it is of a type which should be killed. In any case a clean kill is easiest if the animal is moving slowly past the hunter, and this is always to be sought because a wounded animal might bolt and frighten the deer in the rest of the forest.

The management of the driving teams, including the direction of the drive (which depends on the direction of the wind and the state of the foliage, amongst other things), and the shape of the drive-line is a highly skilled affair. It can only be planned by experienced hunters having complete authority over a driving team of perhaps one hundred men in a big drive. Hugh said that he had only been on six big drives and that each had been planned in detail for several days, the Royal party taking into account all the forester's knowledge of where different types of deer were in the forest, and how they were likely to move when disturbed.

The fourth management task was keeping the deer fit and healthy which depended on the proper farming of all the foodstuffs in the forest, together with the protection of the deer from poachers and other disturbances. Many of the food trees and thickets in the forest had been planted fifty years before and work going on now would stand the deer in good stead fifty years from now. Hugh said he was very proud of the way in which *special vert* (pear trees, crab trees, hawthorns and blackthorn) had been developed throughout his bailiwick and he dwelt for a little on the length of time which infant crabs and pears have to be protected after planting.

He had explained to me at the beginning that the work of a woodsman is mainly with the trees and other plants in the forest, and that he should try to arrange these so that the deer are able to find food throughout the year and also that they have ample cover.

If food supplies are difficult, not only will the deer become thin and inedible, but hunger might drive them out of the forest onto neighbouring farmlands where they will damage the crops.

In the bailiwick were eight large lawns, each of about two acres, which had been carved out of the forest in ancient days to be grazing and resting places for the deer. And there were two other areas of more than fifty acres, rocky and bare of vegetation, where the deer liked to sun themselves in the spring sunshine.

Priest: You have covered a lot of ground very swiftly! I would like to pause and go over a number of points. First, a very elementary question, how did you forest experts, in a wet forest, in a November storm, make a fire? Even with all the prepared tinder and the best flint, I find it difficult to make a fire in my own well-protected house.

Edwin: I always carried at that time flint and tinder in a leather sleeve in my waist band, next to a small knife (which I took from a dead Burgundian), and my coins, but these were no good with everything either very wet or at least damp inside the house as well as outside. Hugh, however, had a small bow and spindle lighter hidden under two flat stones in a corner of the shed, together with a small bundle of thin dry sticks, and in a short time had a small flame which we quickly nursed into a hot fire inside a crude fireplace at one end of the hut. He had also collected some crayfish from a trap in the Planey Brook and these he boiled in an earthenware bowl that was also hidden in the hut.

Priest: What were the hurdles for and how did you manage to help, with only one hand?

Edwin: I asked Hugh that, when he gave us the hurdles to do and he said that a new planting of seedling trees needed protection from grazing animals (not only deer, but farmstock as well), and that the only way to do this was to surround the whole planting with a stout hurdle fence, a method he called banding.

This steady replacement of trees was the only thing that prevented the forest from becoming a wasteland of briars and scrub. Our orders were to limit the unwooded areas to those lawns and rocky places which already existed and to replant any other area which became untreed. For instance if, say, three large oaks were either blown down or sold to a shipyard, the area which was left bare might be as much as one hundred paces square; by proper planting this could contain an attractive stand of young trees in five or six years if animals could be kept away during that time.

Sometimes, instead of trees, a thicket of the kind of bushes the deer liked to browse on was planted, such as hazel, but this too had to be banded if it was not to disappear when it was only a foot or two high.

As to the way I was able to work with my iron hook, I quickly found a way of drawing a withy through the hook as I moved it into the hurdle and it was probably easier than with a normal hand!

Priest: I think I have had enough of your wet day in the

forest and all this wrestling with hurdles. Tell me about other days, but before you do tell me how you were paid for all this hard work.

Edwin: It was set up so that John and I had a small section of the forest in which to run a little business to make money, some of which had to be handed to Hugh. That we did not make too much at the expense of the future of the forest was of course checked, not only by Hugh, but by a verderer who came round at least every month to look for any transgressions against the forest laws so that these could be reported to the local court.

Hugh was himself responsible to the warden, who had the forest in trust from the king, but the whole operation was checked by the verderers, who reported to the court. Furthermore, there were regarders who were supposed to make an overall check every two or three years.

Priest: In what way did you make money from your section of the forest?

Edwin: Without any further permission from Hugh, we were allowed to sell firewood, this being all the wood which a deer would not eat, such as fallen dead wood or trimmings which a deer could gnaw no further. This we sold either in small lots, often carried on our backs as we went home at night, or through a local carrier who would take a load and sell it.

Then we sometimes sold large trees, but this was a much more complicated matter, Hugh having to get permission from the court, which charged a large fee so that there was little to divide between us.

Where roads ran through our section, we charged carters a yearly fee, and this we were allowed to keep as long as we kept the roads in good repair.

And then agistment, the grazing of farm animals, provided us with a steady income during the summer months, although great care had to be taken to make sure that the farm animals did no permanent damage to the newly growing plantings and coppices.

APPENDIX TWO

Translator's Comments on the Use of Coins in the Twelfth Century

As the reader will have seen how easily life went on without 'money' in the times about which I have written, I want to add a word or two about how money was regarded then.

It seems to me that the countryman looked upon coin as a nest egg, wealth that took up small space and could be easily hidden from prying eyes (unlike most of his other possessions), and his aim was to leave this nest egg (if it existed) untouched.

He was keenly aware of the weakness of coin – that you could never be sure, from day to day, what it would buy, whereas the value of produce, in barter terms, was part of his everyday life. The value of a side of bacon, as food, seemed to him to be obvious to everyone, whereas the amount of food which could be bought with a groat was never obvious. And, of course, with money the bargaining had to be done twice, once when a piece of produce was sold and once when other produce was bought with the money.

But the King had to have coin, not only for his mercenaries but to pay for his overseas adventures, for bribes and payments to ambassadors, for quick purchases in times of shortages and to pay his haughty armourers.

So from the multitude of barters in the countryside had to be squeezed out some coin for the King and, not surprisingly, the country folk connected coin with a process of taxation. There was also a feeling that the making, transfer and storing of coin involved a lot of wasteful expense.

In barter, while bargaining was always involved, there was throughout the countryside a good understanding of the 'value' of commodities. The only change in values came about through that self-same bargaining, in which, except in times of plague or famine, movement took place slowly.

Dorothy Rowe in her book, *The Real Meaning of Money*, gives three examples to show how easily a money economy can slip back into a barter economy. Her first example is that the seventeenth century settlers in America quickly slipped into commodities such as 'dried fish, furs, gunpowder and wampum – Indian beads made from the inside of seashells' when their supply of coins was used up. And secondly the British settlers in Australia 'turned to a much prized possession, rum, to serve as money'. Her third example is much more recent, in the 1980s, when bartering systems known as Local Exchange Trading Systems (LETS) grew up in Britain with different districts having a distinctive name for its 'money'. Thus Manchester would call its 'money' 'bobbins', and Exmouth, 'cockles'.

Finally, it took a long time for money to be formed into a reliable, reproducible means of exchange. Eileen Power in her fascinating book, *Medieval People*, notes that even in the fifteenth century, a wool exporter in London, Thomas Betson (wool being by far England's chief export at that time), 'had difficulties... when into his counting house there wandered in turn the Andrew guilder of Scotland, the Arnoldus Gulden of Gueldres (very much debased), the Carolus groat of Charles of Burgundy, new crowns and old crowns of France, the David and the Falewe of the Bishopric of Utrecht, the Hettinus groat of the Counts of Westphalia, the Lewe or French Louis d'or the Limburg groat, the Milan groat, the Nimueguen groat, the Phelippus or Philippe d'or of Brabant, the Plaques of Utrecht, the Postlates of various Bishops, the English Ryall, (worth ten shillings), the Scots Rider or the Rider of Burgundy, (so called because they bore the figure of a man on horseback) the Florin

Rhenau of the Bishopric of Cologne, and the Setillers. He had to know the value in English money of them all... and most of them were debased past all reason'.

Perhaps it becomes clearer how our present day moneyers have grown up accustomed to such large commissions on all exchanges!

Bibliography

Briggs, Asa, *A Social History of England*, Book Club Associates

Chibnall, Marjorie, *Anglo-Norman England 1066-1166*, Basil Blackwell

Churchill, Winston S, *A History of the English Speaking Peoples, Vol I, The Birth of Britain*, Cassell & Co Ltd

Duby, Georges (Ed), *A History of Private Life, II Revelations of the Medieval World*, Belknap Press of Harvard University Press

Elkins, Sharon K, *Holy Women of 12th Century England*, University of N Carolina Press

Gurevich A J, *Categories of Medieval Cultures*, Routledge and Kegan Paul

Hindle, B P, 'Seasonal Variations in Travel in Medieval England', *Journal of Transport History*, Vol 3

Kealey, Edward J, *Harvesting the Air, Windmill Pioneers in Twelfth Century England*, The Boydell Press

Knoop, Douglas, & Jones J P, *The Medieval Mason*, Manchester University Press

Marcus Aurelius, *Meditations*, Trans by George Long, Collins

Mariarty, Catherine (Ed), *The Voice of the Middle Ages, Personal Letters 1100-1500*, Lennard Publishing

Martin G H, 'Road Travel in the Middle Ages', *Journal of Transport History*, Vols 4-5

Potter K R, *Gesta Stephani* – translated from the Latin, Thomas Nelson & Son Ltd

Power, Eileen, *Medieval People*, Methuen & Co Ltd

Pythian-Adams, Charles,*Continuity, Fields and Fissions: The Making of a Midland Parish*, Lancaster University Press

Rackham, Oliver, *The History of the Countryside*, J M Dent & Sons Ltd

Rowe, Dorothy, *The Real Meaning of Money*, Harper Collins

Scott-Giles, C W (Compiler), *The Road Goes On*, The Epworth Press

Stafford, Pauline, *The East Midlands in the Early Middle Ages*, Leicester University Press

Stiefel, Tina, *The Intellectual Revolution in Twelfth Century Europe*, Croom Helm

Swanton, Michael (Trans & Ed), *The Anglo-Saxon Chronicle*, J M Dent

Tyerman, Christopher (Series Ed Geoffrey Treasure), *Who's Who in Medieval England*, Shepheard-Walwyn

Wilson, Frederick,*Arms and Armour*, Hamlyn Publishing Grp Ltd

Young, Charles R, *The Royal Forest of Medieval England*, Leicester University Press